JOOP

Also by Richard Lourie

FICTION

The Autobiography of Joseph Stalin

Zero Gravity

First Loyalty

Sagittarius in Warsaw

NONFICTION

Sakharov: A Biography

Hunting the Devil

Russia Speaks: An Oral History from the Revolution to the Present

Predicting Russia's Future

Letters to the Future

SELECTED TRANSLATIONS

Visions from San Francisco Bay by Czeslaw Milosz

Memoirs by Andrei Sakharov

The Life and Extraordinary Adventures of Private Ivan Chonkin by Vladimir Voinovich

Goodnight! by Abram Tertz (Andrei Sinyavsky)

My Century by Aleksander Wat

JOOP
A Novel of Anne Frank

Richard Lourie

THOMAS DUNNE BOOKS
St. Martin's Griffin ❦ New York

This is a work of fiction. All of the characters, organizations, and events portrayed in this novel are either products of the author's imagination or are used fictitiously.

THOMAS DUNNE BOOKS.
An imprint of St. Martin's Press.

JOOP. Copyright © 2007 by Richard Lourie. All rights reserved. Printed in the United States of America. For information, address St. Martin's Press, 175 Fifth Avenue, New York, N.Y. 10010.

www.thomasdunnebooks.com
www.stmartins.com

Design by Kathryn Parise

Library of Congress Cataloging-in-Publication Data

Lourie, Richard, 1940–
    [Hatred for tulips]
    Joop: a novel of Anne Frank / Richard Lourie.—1st St. Martin's Griffin ed.
      p. cm.
    Originally published: A hatred for tulips. New York: Thomas Dunne Books. 2007.
    "Thomas Dunne Books."
    ISBN-13: 978-0-312-38587-3 (pbk.)
    ISBN-10: 0-312-38587-0 (pbk.)
    1. Frank, Anne, 1929–1945—Fiction. 2. Autobiographical memory—Fiction. 3. Betrayal—Fiction. 4. World War, 1939–1945—Fiction. 5. Jews—Persecutions—Fiction. I. Title.

PS3562.O833 H38 2008
813'.54—dc22

2008029755

First published by St. Martin's Press as *A Hatred for Tulips*

First St. Martin's Griffin Edition: October 2008

10 9 8 7 6 5 4 3 2 1

For Helen Rees, the agent of this book in more ways than one, and to James Salter and Jod for the gift of harsh critique

Fiction is history that didn't happen and history is fiction that did.
GEORGE ORWELL

PART I

1

"I am your brother," said the stranger at the door.

At first I thought he was one of those evangelicals who go from house to house peddling salvation, but then I looked more closely at his face and saw my mother's eyes looking back at me.

"Come in," I said.

We didn't fall into each other's arms or even shake hands, one too much, the other too little. We hadn't seen each other for sixty years. What did it mean that we were brothers?

I held the door open for him and as I watched him walk past in profile, I thought: Willem must be sixty-five now.

But he didn't look it. A face that hadn't seen much. A gray-haired boy. An American.

"I don't have much to offer you," I said. "Beer. Some ham, cheese, bread."

"Sounds good."

"I live alone. I don't keep much in the house."

"You never married?" he asked, sounding concerned.

"No."

I didn't ask him about himself. Didn't have to.

"I was lucky," he said. "Found the right woman and found her early. Two kids. Five grandchildren. My oldest, Cindy—"

"I'll be back in a minute with the beer."

I didn't want to hear their names, see their snapshots. Willem had gotten everything. When our mother left our father for a Canadian soldier at the end of the war, it was young Willem she took with her and so he'd gotten everything, her, a family, America.

"Dutch beer is the best," he said after a good swig.

"You like a drink then?"

"Since I first tried it."

"It's in the blood then," I said with a smile and he smiled too, though I knew we had to be smiling for different reasons.

"You must be sixty-five, Willem," I said.

"That's right," he said. "I am. I don't know where the time went, the years just flew by."

I knew he was speaking about his own life, how one day you wake up old, but he was also apologizing for never having come to see his own brother in all those sixty years since our mother took him from Holland.

"What was your work, Willem?"

"I was an optometrist. You?"

"I worked in the food industry like my father. Our father. You must excuse if I sometimes say 'my father' and not 'our father.' I've been saying it so long."

"Sure," said Willem, with a look of pain on his face that I was glad to see, "sure, I understand."

"But I wasn't a cook like *our* father. I worked in wholesale, warehousing, distribution."

"Retired?"

"For several years."

I knew he was about to ask me what I did with my time but was somehow reluctant to. Maybe sitting across from me at the table, he could see into me a little.

People who don't have secrets imagine them as dark and hidden. It's just the opposite. Secrets are bright. They light you up. Like the bare lightbulb left on in a cell day and night, they give you no rest.

In a way I'm amazed that he couldn't see into me, I feel so transparent.

Or maybe he was just having second thoughts about coming over here, coming to see me. He was clearly a little uncomfortable in my place, which was clean but dingy.

We finished the first beer with small talk—how was the flight over, what hotel was he staying in, how long did he intend to stay in Amsterdam?

"At least a week," he said. "I mean, there's a lot to see and do. And I promised the grandkids to make a video of everything for them. One of them's doing a 'My Heritage' project for school, the one I started to tell you about, Cindy . . . wait a second, I want to show you something. Tell me," he said, pulling his wallet out from his back pocket and flipping it open to the snapshot section, "tell me Cindy doesn't look just like our mother."

Now I hated him. It was our mother reborn as an American

teenager and though the hair was done up in an American style, it was still our mother's thick, blond hair, and her eyes were the same too, she even had the same green vein at the side of her temple. So, not only did he get to have our mother for all his childhood, he got to have her again as a grandchild.

But I must not be transparent in any way—at least, he didn't seem to notice. "Cindy's a terrific kid, kind, helpful, full of good, clean fun. And of all the kids and grandkids, she's the one who's most interested in her Dutch background. Reads everything she can get her hands on."

"You should have brought her over."

"Maybe next time," he said with what seemed a kind of wistful sadness. Maybe he had some serious illness, I thought, maybe that's why he's decided to make the trip and see his brother, though he still hasn't once called me by name.

"She should come," I said. "Holland has plenty to offer. But teach her one thing from her uncle."

"What's that?"

"Not to *ooh* and *aah* over the tulips. I hate tulips. They're too pretty when they're alive and look so dead when they die. But the real reason I hate them is I know what they taste like. In the war, at the end, when there was nothing, we ate them, we ate tulip bulbs."

"I don't remember that," he said. "I don't remember much. And the few memories I do have, I can't be sure if they're really true or just stories my mother, our mother, told me."

"You're lucky then."

"But I want to know what happened. During the war. And just after."

"What for?"

"You know the feeling when someone starts to tell you a good story, then right after he gets going he decides he shouldn't be telling it and just stops. And you try to convince him that once you start a story, you have to finish, it isn't fair otherwise. Most people will give in to that but sometimes they won't and you're left completely frustrated. Well, that's sort of how I feel about my life, except it's the beginning I don't know about."

"And that's why you came here?"

"That's why I came here, Joop."

"Well, maybe you can tell me a few stories too."

"Maybe I can."

"Except for a few postcards from our mother and the letter you sent when she died, there's not much I know."

"I know," he said, dropping his eyes. "I'm sorry."

"Another beer?"

"Another beer would be good."

For a second in the kitchen I did not want to go back to the table, to my brother, to the past and all its sorrows.

I looked out the window. The sky was a bright blue with a few gray rain clouds. A young woman pedaled by on a black bike, talking on her cell phone.

If I had died three years ago in the hospital, none of this would have happened, my brother, the rain cloud, the girl on her bike. But I didn't die.

I went back to the front room.

My brother took a long swig of beer. The part of the story he did know—our mother leaving our father, who had been in-capacitated by a stroke right after the war—wasn't too pretty, and the part he didn't know about wasn't any prettier.

Take a good swig, my lucky American brother, who has so

few bad memories that he had to come all the way to Holland to get some.

"You know who Anne Frank is?" I asked.

"Of course," he said, as if I had offended his intelligence and Dutch pride.

"When they came to get her, they went right to her hiding place."

"I know."

"And that means someone betrayed her."

"But who did it?" he said.

"You."

2

Just listen, just listen, I'll tell you everything.

I'm going to call our father "my father" because you weren't even born yet. And so, my father was a gloomy bastard when sober but he sweetened up when drinking. I'm the same way.

When I was a boy, I was always glad to see him pouring himself something to drink. Just by watching I learned how long each drink took to sweeten him up. The lighter the color, the quicker.

I'd pass by the door to the kitchen and take a quick look to see if his face had brightened up yet. Then I'd go over to him. But never before.

Otherwise, he might just bat me away. He wasn't big but he had strong hands covered with burns and cuts.

One day I asked him the name of the brown drink.

"Beer," he said, always glad when I asked him the name of any food or drink.

"It makes you happy too slow."

For a second he looked puzzled by what I said, and I was afraid I had made him angry. But then he smiled and put his arm around me and pulled me over.

"Pretty damn smart, Joop," he said. I always liked it when he called me by name.

Love and praise together, that was rare.

"Yes," he said, "beer *is* slower. But it's nice to drink. You know who invented it?"

"Who?"

"The Egyptians. The same ones that built the Pyramids."

It didn't seem possible to me that those mysterious people I always pictured moving sideways could have invented beer. But since my father said it, it was true.

He knew everything about food and drink. He was a hotel chef and proud of his profession. He had apprenticed in France and liked to talk about that. In one French kitchen where he worked there was a sign that said, YOU HAVE CHOSEN A NOBLE PROFESSION. Sometimes he said it in French—*"Vous avez choisi un métier noble"*—because the sound of the words made him remember those days.

Not that he liked the French. "Cheapest bastards in the world."

That day my father pointed to his glass. "Try it, Joop," he said. "Take a sip."

I gave him a quick look to see if he meant it. He nodded.

I picked up the glass with both hands so as not to spill a drop and spoil the mood. It tasted like bitter wheat.

I told him I liked it but he laughed because he could see my twisted lips.

I grabbed the glass and took a long sip, which made him laugh again but in a different way.

A little later I went outside. I don't know what it was, the time with him, the beer, but for a few minutes everything, the canal, the trees, the sky, was like a stained glass window with the light pouring through. As if God had come close to the other side of the sky and noticed me.

I loved my mother when she sang along with the radio and when she was good to me, but I hated her when she was mean to my father. I didn't always understand what she was saying to him but I could always hear the anger or, worse, the contempt. Of course, she was good to him when he was taking her out or giving her money. She loved to go out and dress well. Sometimes she talked about herself as if she were another person: "You got the prettiest girl in the school and she doesn't want to wear housedresses all the time."

If my father had been drinking, he would just laugh it off and say, "And she's still the prettiest. But I'm not taking her out . . . until she buys a new dress." And he'd push some guilders across the table.

But if he hadn't had anything to drink, his head would slump until he finally raised it in a fury, swearing a blue streak. In all my life I never heard anyone who could swear like him.

Then they'd fight, shout, throw things. I'd always go outside, squeezing my way past the bicycles in the front hall.

I can still remember the door clicking shut behind me, in

front of me the brick houses, the bare trees, the canals frozen with people skating on them. I wanted to skate away with them and never come back.

But I'd forget about it the next time my father talked to me. "Even the Queen wakes up hungry," my father used to say with gusto. I never quite understood what he meant. Of course the Queen wakes up hungry, she's been sleeping and hasn't had anything to eat. Then I saw that the clue was in the extra word "even." The Queen was the most special person but even she woke up hungry, which meant that even she was like everyone else. The whole world woke up hungry. And so my father had chosen the world's best job.

I told him all that and he said, "Joop, tomorrow you're coming with me."

The next day he took me to the food markets. The tomatoes looked even more red all piled up. My father showed me how to tell the different types of fish and which were the good ones to buy.

The vendors all greeted him, some because they liked him, some just because he bought from them. He introduced me as "my son, Joop," "my boy, Joop."

"And what do you think the Queen had for breakfast today?" he asked.

"Milk and tomatoes."

He laughed and bought us some fresh herring and a couple of his favorite sandwiches, beef tartare on a bun. He drank a beer with his but didn't offer me any even though I was bigger now and had already had some. Still, it was another happy time. And we walked home slow.

3

There was still orange bunting on the trees from the Queen's birthday on the day the war started. A nice summer's day. I was outside playing. People's windows were open. Then I heard something different, wrong—shouts, loud radios. I ran into the house.

My mother was pacing back and forth with a dishrag in one hand that she kept pulling on with the other. The radio was crackling.

"What is it?" I said.

"A war."

"Will the soldiers come here?"

For a second she didn't say anything. "No, they won't come here."

Later that day, her brother, my uncle Frans, came over. He tried to calm my mother down. "The Polish pigs won't last a week and then things will quiet back down."

But she didn't believe him. "You think that's all Hitler wants?"

"I've read his book. If he goes for anything else, it'll be the Russian Communists. He's headed east, he'll keep east."

That seemed to satisfy her.

I had heard Hitler's name on the radio and from the grown-ups talking.

"Uncle Frans, why are the Germans killing Polish pigs, don't they have any pigs of their own?"

He laughed in a way that I hated. I felt stupid and embarrassed. But it was my own fault. I should have waited and asked my father. I had somehow betrayed my father to that laughing fool of an uncle who was now even making my mother laugh, though for that I was glad.

"No, no," he said, "the Poles aren't pigs, they're people."

That made me want to ask more questions but I wasn't about to ask him.

I went back outside again, the door clicking shut behind me.

I saw the boy from next door, who was younger than me and always did what I said.

"Let's play war."

"Let's."

"You're the pig people and I'm the Hitler."

"Oink, oink," he said and ran off behind a tree.

We played for a while then his mother came and scooped him up. I didn't care. He was too young to be much fun to play with and all I really wanted to do was talk with my father. But I didn't know when I'd see him. He came home late and slept late and I saw him only on his days off.

I was in school and did pretty good. I had a little group of chums, some for soccer, some just for talking and fooling around. Ours was a pretty good group. Not the best, but pretty good. Every kid knows what the best group is. And the worst. Kids tried to get into our group, but we didn't take many.

When I went back in the house, Uncle Frans was gone and my mother was scrubbing the kitchen with a fury. I went to my room and got out my picture book of the world. Every country was a different color—Holland was orange, Germany green, Poland brown, and Russia light yellow. Holland was by far the smallest of the four. The Germans had gone into Poland, which was away from Holland. Uncle Frans had said that, if anything, the Germans would keep going in that direction, and my mother had said no soldiers would come here. The only problem was that we were right next door to Germany. Uncle Frans and my mother were probably right but I wouldn't feel a hundred percent sure until I talked with my father.

It happened two days later.

"And how was school today?" he said, pouring himself a third drink of clear liquor.

"Very good. Only two other boys could answer more questions than me."

"They must be Jews."

"Why?"

"They think they're smarter than anybody else, smarter than dumb Dutchmen."

"Dutchmen aren't dumb!"

"My little patriot." He rubbed my hair.

"So, are the Jews bad like some people say?"

"It's not that they're so bad, it'd just be better if they weren't around. But Catholics are worse."

"Why did Hitler attack the Poles?"

"You want to know the real answer?"

"Yes."

"The real answer is that Hitler is crazy and nobody ever knows why he's doing what he does."

"Who's worse, Hitler or the Jews?"

"It's all the same, Hitler, the Jews, the Communists, they make trouble and don't let you live."

"Who are the Communists?"

"Russians who want to take away everything you have and work you like a slave."

"Will the Americans help?"

"Maybe this time they'll say, 'So, people are killing each other in Europe again, who cares?' That's the main thing about this world, son, people kill each other and no one cares."a

4

My talk with my father left me with two different feelings. I was glad and proud that he had talked to me like a big boy about the world. But the world he talked to me about seemed a crazy, dangerous place where things could change suddenly in a second. Hitler could scream and make his armies turn around and head right for Holland. And then people would kill each other here and no one would care.

We talked about it in the schoolyard. Everyone had a different idea depending on what their father had told them. One boy said that Hitler would not attack us because *Deutsch* and Dutch were like cousins. Another boy said that if the Germans came, they would only take the Jews and Communists and leave the good Dutchmen alone. And I said that Hitler was so crazy he might even come and take all the Dutchmen and just leave the Jews and the Communists.

Then a strange thing happened. There were a few Jews in our school. One always got teased. He had black curly hair that looked oily and so he was easy to spot. I'd heard kids calling him "Jew." A few times I even thought of yelling "Jew" at him just to see what would happen. But I never got the chance, I stopped seeing him around. At first I thought he might be sick, but after a couple of days I heard that he had moved to England. Just suddenly gone. Poof!

Weeks passed, nothing happened. People began talking about other things, the adults about prices and money, the boys about when the canals would freeze over, next summer's Olympics. Still, I could see some changes. My father grumbled that people weren't coming to the restaurant; my mother was now either distracted or affectionate, where before she had not been much of either.

I didn't know she was pregnant until her belly got big in the late fall. My father would pat her there but I could see that sometimes he was only doing it to make her feel good.

The twins, I mean you and Jan, were born just after the new year. While my mother was in the hospital, my father took me with him to the markets again. He walked more slowly and examined the food more closely. "Lean times sharpen the eye." I didn't know how times could be lean and didn't like the idea of eyes being sharpened.

The vendors talked to him in a different way now, some less friendly, some more.

"You a father again?" asked one of them from behind his ice and herring.

"Twice over."

"Twins?"

"Boys."

"At least it's boys."

"Yes, but she'll still be wanting a girl to dress up."

I knew how babies were made by then. I'd heard them at it, even caught sight of them a few times. The wildness of it scared me and excited me at the same time. One kid at school knew everything about it, except that people moved when doing it. No one had told him and he'd never caught his parents at it. So when he found out that people moved, he was dumbfounded. We laughed about that one for days.

Winter came, the canals froze. There was plenty of lousy Dutch weather and people enjoyed grumbling about it more than usual, as a change from talking about the war.

"Do armies fight in the winter?" I asked my father.

"Only if they have to. People would rather kill each other in the nice weather."

We were safe till spring.

5

Everything changed when you twins came home. A new baby is always special and twins are twice that. They had all the attention of my parents, my relatives, anyone who came over.

I hated you two. What were you—lumps of flesh in a blanket. My poor mother never got any sleep. If one twin was sleeping, the other one would start crying and wake the first one up. Then for a while you twins began falling asleep at exactly the same time and waking up at exactly the same time. People talked about that too.

"They're like the same person in two bodies."

"Wait till they grow, they'll play tricks on you, one pretending to be the other."

"And some of them have powers too," said an old woman, without any doubt in her voice. "They can send thoughts through the air and break a teacup without touching it. Seen it myself."

One day my mother laid you two down on her bed and said to me, "Watch the twins for a second, I have to wash my hands. Don't let them roll off the bed."

It was the first time I was really alone with the two of you and I brought my face down close to see what was so special about you. My eyes looked right into your eyes, the same slate blue eyes all babies have. You two started howling at the same time.

My mother ran in and pushed me aside with wet hands.

"What did you do to them?"

"Nothing. Just looked at them."

She picked you two up and carried you out of the room, leaving me alone by the bed where she had made the two of you with my father.

You twins never liked me after that. You had secret ways of communicating with each other, little looks, little moves of your fingers. And you had secret ways of communicating with me too. Even though you couldn't talk, I could hear you two telling me, "We don't like you but we'll pretend to so not to make our mother sad. And you have to pretend to like us too, *if* you love your mother."

I always knew something bad was bound to happen with you two, I just didn't know what. I tried to stay as far from you as possible. If something happened, I didn't want to be blamed. I even had the feeling you wanted something to happen so that I would be blamed and you could have our mother's love all to yourselves. One time I was walking down the cellar stairs when all of a sudden I tripped and fell. I was sure you made me do it; you could send your thoughts through the air and break cups, couldn't you?

Guests, relatives, and neighbors were always asking me how I liked having twin brothers. I knew what I was supposed to say and I said it. They didn't even bother to look at my face to see if I was lying, as any kid would; they really weren't interested and only cared that I said the right thing.

But Uncle Frans noticed. "I remember when my sister, your mother, was born; it was like I'd been robbed, like someone just came by and snatched my favorite toy out of my hand."

For the first time since you two had come home I felt free and at peace. I could never have this talk with my father and never suspected that I could have it with anyone else.

"And she was born pretty too," Uncle Frans went on. "You had to love her. But you got it different."

Even though I always felt I should never ask any important question to anyone but my father, still I asked Uncle Frans, "Just what are twins?"

I could see him pause because it was a hard question and he wanted to give me a good answer. "Twins aren't like freak babies, born without arms and legs, but you can't say they're one hundred percent normal either. What we look like, the color of our eyes, the shape of our hands, our abilities, it all comes to us from the blood. People get their identities through the blood, and so do nations. You must never betray your blood."

"Isn't that what the Germans say?"

"The Germans aren't stupid. Just look around you. In some families everyone can sing, in some families no one can carry a tune. In some families no one takes a drink, in other families everybody's got a glass in their hand. Why? Because some blood likes the taste of alcohol and some blood doesn't."

"Mine doesn't."

"Yours will."

But it wasn't so much what he said that day that mattered as that I had discovered something—you could have a private understanding with another person.

Of course I had my friends at school to talk to. I told them, "The twins are mean and selfish and hate me because they have to share their mother with me. And they're very smart and have powers that regular people don't have."

"Like what?"

"Like breaking teacups without touching them; an old lady saw it, I heard her say."

Uncle Frans had joined the Dutch Nazis, the National Socialists, and wore an NSB armband. "Good or bad, I don't know," he said, "but great times are coming. Real history!"

"History is nothing but trouble," said my father. "I don't like it."

"You think history cares if you like it?"

"To hell with history."

I felt strange listening to them talk. I felt connected to both of them now. And it felt wrong for my father not to know Uncle Frans and I had spoken.

Uncle Frans had some good ideas. He thought about things, he read the papers. But I was glad my father got the last word.

And anyway, Uncle Frans was wrong, Hitler didn't keep

marching east. Early in the morning of another nice day, May 10, '40, the Germans arrived. By land and air. A few days of fighting, Rotterdam bombed to the ground, surrender. The Germans put up their own street signs, black and yellow.

The Queen fled to England, the same place the Jew from my school went. It seemed impossible. How could the Queen leave her country? It was like your own mother running away. But that's what war does. It makes impossible things possible. And it does it so often it makes them routine. Like starvation. Like sending children to their death.

6

But then all of a sudden the Germans couldn't have been nicer. They rose to give up their seats to old people on the trams, always paid for everything in the stores, never shouted. Dutch girls started going out with them. Most people didn't like that.

Uncle Frans said the Germans were showing us a better life, that Hitler had raised them from the Depression and would do the same for us. And there was more work now, more money.

All the boys cared about was whether the war would cancel the Olympics. Holland had done pretty well in the '36 Olympics in Berlin. "Tinus" Osendarp had been only two-tenths of a second behind Jesse Owens in the 100-meter dash—two-tenths! And six-tenths behind him in the 200. "Rie" Mastenbroek took the gold in the women's free-style swimming and we were proud of that, though of course it mattered more to the girls.

And we had also won in two very Dutch sports—sailing and cycling.

I had one friend at school, Kees, we tried out the bad things together, smoking, spitting, and swearing.

"What can the Germans do to kids?" I asked him.

"Whatever they want."

"And what can kids do to Germans?"

"That's a good question," said Kees. "We better think about it."

I always had the good questions. Kees was braver, even when caught. You could make him cry but never beg. He had bristly white-blond hair and eyebrows the same color, which made his eyes look like clear blue marbles.

"We could put sand in their gas tanks," I said as we were walking the alleyways near the port. "I read about that." He smiled. We were on. We went out to the Damrak to scout around. Most of the traffic now was German Army trucks, very few cars, still plenty of bicycles; they hadn't been requisitioned yet. The trams were still running.

There was a bunch of German trucks by the train station, some with their motors running, some turned off. Germans soldiers stood around, smoking, talking. They were mostly young, and happy with their easy victory. They paid little attention to us. And when one of them did look at us, we smiled, pretending to admire their uniforms and guns.

We slipped behind a row of trucks. They had yellowish spring mud on their tires, which were almost as tall as we were. The gas caps didn't look easy to open.

Most of the German soldiers may have been happy and polite, but there's always a mean one and he found us soon enough.

"Get out of where you don't belong!" he hissed.

"Go study your German," said one of the soldiers as we walked away fast, but without running.

"*Kennst du das Land . . . ,*" another one started singing.

We didn't give up, though. We started collecting sand and dirt in our bookpacks, which we wore on our backs.

"How much do you think it will take to clog up an engine?" I asked Kees.

"For a German engine, a lot," he said.

Then school was out and we wouldn't be seeing each other every day. We swapped telephone numbers, promising not to say a word of our plans over the line.

We met fairly often during that first summer of the war. It was a good summer, except there were no Olympics. And for me and Kees it was a very good summer. I played hard and my bones grew. And on top of everything else we had our own secret game.

Sometimes I felt I should tell my father, ask my father. But I could barely get through to him, and asking his permission would probably just make him angrier. And besides, I could always tell him later when he couldn't do anything about it and would just be proud of me. Still, I was worried I'd taken the coward's way out.

Collecting sand, dirt, and gravel wasn't the problem. The problem was finding a truck that was left alone long enough for us to get the gas cap off and the dirt in.

We walked the streets of the city from Westermarkt to Weesperplein. We wore down our soles and heels, and soon enough the cobblers would be closing down; no glue, they'd say, no shoe leather either.

To save time, when we finally did find the right truck, Kees had made a funnel out of a magazine and some twine to pour the dirt right in.

Weeks passed. We kept trudging. Our packs felt even heavier in the hot sun and we started to get discouraged. "I've got the worst goddamned luck in the world!" I said, using one of my father's favorite expressions.

"Only takes one," said Kees, but not sounding like he much meant it.

Then for a while neither of us would call the other or if we saw each other, we wouldn't talk about our plan and just play whatever game the other boys were playing. Summer's one long day when you're a kid and we thought we had nothing but time. Then all of a sudden that day starts coming to a close and it's almost schooltime again. We both started feeling ashamed of ourselves for being bigger than our britches.

Then without any discussion, we started hunting for the perfect truck again. All we had to do now was keep at it and our luck would change. But soon that hot, discouraged feeling started coming back, the straps of our bookpacks digging into our skin. But we hated the idea of giving up.

All it took was one corner to change our luck, a little street off Raamstraat, not far from police headquarters. A German jeep was parked half on the sidewalk, half on the street, like they'd run out in a hurry. There wasn't a soul in sight except for an old lady in a butcher shop.

"We can't waste a second," said Kees, starting to wriggle out of his pack as he trotted toward the jeep. I ran ahead to start to work on the gas cap. There was a warm diesel smell around the jeep, which meant that it hadn't been there long and so they might not be coming back right away.

The gas cap wouldn't budge for me. I tried both hands. Nothing.

Kees bumped me aside. He was stronger, not a lot, but some. I didn't want him doing everything so I started wriggling out of my pack as fast as I could, but one arm got caught in a strap and I felt like a fool.

"I can't do it either," said Kees. "Maybe the two of us."

So I had to run over with one arm still tangled in the strap.

"Two hands, two hands," said Kees. "Use both."

"I'm trying, I'm trying."

That was as far as we got. I felt a hand grip my shoulder hard and I whispered, "Kees."

I could barely make my head turn around. The first thing I saw was the NSB armband of the Dutch Nazis and the next was the face of Uncle Frans.

"I thought I saw my nephew a few blocks back. And I said to myself, I know him, he's got no books in his pack. And now I can see my stupid little nephew's playing at sabotage."

He smacked our heads and kicked us in the ass as we went running.

That was the end of the Dutch resistance. Mine, anyway.

7

My mother wasn't answering the door anymore. The days when the greengrocer and the dairy man came around to the house were over now. And the people who did come to our door never brought anything good. She didn't like the world anymore. Before, she had always been haranguing my father to go out, now the front door made her afraid.

If I was home, she'd send me to the door unless she was expecting someone at a certain hour. But I didn't like going to the door either. I kept expecting to see Uncle Frans. I was afraid he'd give me another crack on the head and drag me in to tell my parents what danger I'd put the family in.

Sometimes my mother would tell my father to answer the door. She used a different voice with him, more reproachful—"at least make yourself useful."

He was home even more now. Still working a few days a week, but the restaurant was only being kept alive by the German officers who ate there. "Any job is better than no job," he'd say to my mother, "but I hate feeding the bastards." And he'd add: "A noble profession." Now it didn't matter what color liquor my father drank, nothing seemed to brighten him up.

Some people did make more money now but most of them weren't spending it in restaurants. People were afraid the Germans would change the way they treated us and take our money. In fact, later on the Germans did confiscate Dutch coins for the silver and nickel they contained and replaced them with tinny Nazi Dutch coins. They put tulips on the ten-cent coin; everybody hated that.

Since he was home more, my mother tried to make my father help with the twins: "I was never supposed to be the mother of twins. It's too much for me. All I wanted was a daughter."

"We take what we're sent," my father would say.

"Then let them send us some guilders."

One day there was a hard knock on the door and she told me to go get it. My heart was racing. This time I was sure it was Uncle Frans just by the hardness of the knock.

I was almost right. It was another Dutch Nazi, selling the NSB rag *People and Country*. They did it to raise money and spread their ideas, of course, but they also wanted to see who turned them down. And they let you know they wouldn't forget.

This one was short and fat, the angry, stupid kind, always afraid they're being laughed at, always afraid they're being tricked.

I was so relieved it wasn't Uncle Frans that I even smiled as I said, "My uncle's in the NSB, he brings the paper round." For good measure, I threw in: "And then we talk it over."

He looked right at me to see if I was lying, but since half of what I said was true my face must have looked all right.

"Very good," he said and went on to bother the next person.

It was the first time I had ever been proud to lie. Protecting my mother, who would only be upset by dealing with someone like him. But the good feeling didn't last long. I started to worry—what if the newspaperman knows Uncle Frans and tells him what I said, then Uncle Frans would have more sticks to beat me with.

And so the next time there was a knock at the door I was twice as scared.

"Go see who it is," my mother called from the kitchen, where she was feeding the twins porridge while humming along to music on the radio.

This time the knock was not as sharp as the other day, but Uncle Frans was the tricky sort, he might knock soft to fool you.

As soon as I had opened up the door even a little I could see that it wasn't Uncle Frans or any other grown-up.

It was Maarten, a big boy from up the street. He was one of the best athletes, everyone liked him. Older than me, he would never speak to anyone my age.

"*Razzia* for copper," he said with a nod, which meant nod back if you know *razzia* means raid. I nodded back.

I was proud that Maarten had spoken to me—and to entrust me with something of importance, that was really something. But I also felt ashamed because my own attempt at resistance had only led to a kick in the ass and me living in constant fear of Uncle Frans.

"Who was that?" my mother asked when I came back into the kitchen.

"*Razzia* for copper," I said, proud to inform her that her son had been entrusted with such important information.

But proud is not what she felt. My mother looked away and started crying, and a second later the twins started too. I just stood there with the radio playing and them crying and my father not home when we could have used him. Then, all of a sudden, like I knew what I was doing, I grabbed the copper fruit bowl from the table and took it out back to the potting shed where my parents kept their tools and bulbs, the tulips bulbs we'd end up boiling to eat. I hid it behind a pile of wood and clay pots and even arranged things on top to make you not want to take the pile apart.

"Don't worry, I hid it," I said when I went back in.

By now my mother had stopped crying and was paying total attention to feeding the twins and didn't make any answer. I knew it was better not to say anything else.

I went to the front of the house to wait for the knock at the door that would mean that the *razzia* had come.

I was getting myself ready to lie again. But this time it would be harder. A *razzia* was not the same as a guy selling newspapers. In a *razzia* you could tell the truth and they still wouldn't believe you. They'd burst right in.

The longer I waited, the faster my pulse raced. And the faster it raced, the more confused I got. Now I knew I couldn't even lie to them. I was afraid that if they started shouting and slapping me around, I'd blurt out where I hid the copper bowl. Then I'd put the family in even more danger because it would mean that I'd been warned about the *razzia* and had disobeyed

German orders. Now there were more counts against me—disobedience, sabotage, and lying to the NSB newspaperman.

But in the end nothing happened that day. In a war nothing is predictable, not even the violence. It's coming, it's coming, then all of a sudden it veers off somewhere else.

We talked a lot about the war at school. Now we didn't just repeat what our fathers had been saying, we all had some experience of our own to go by.

"I saw a couple of German soldiers the other day so skinny any Dutchman could take them in a fair fight."

"Some of them are all right. One gave me candy."

"They're under orders to be nice to the Dutch and that'll change if the orders change."

"Some people say the Germans will go soon and attack the Russians."

"So how come they went east first, then turned around and came here?"

"First they had to beat Poland and establish a base, then come here to resupply themselves before they go after the Russians."

"But isn't Holland supposed to be neutral?"

"The Germans don't give a shit."

Kees wasn't in my class that year but I saw him on the playground. For a while we didn't say anything to each other because we were still ashamed about getting caught and kicked in the ass. But then we got bored with not talking and started up again.

"Did you get in trouble?" he asked.

"Not yet."

"Me neither. I know some kids who do warnings about *razzias.*"

"You know Maarten, he came to our house. But aren't they all older than us?"

"There's a couple our age. But they only want the best ones, who can run fast and lie good."

"I'm better at lying now. And pretty fast."

"Me too," said Kees, who was better at both.

"Can you ask them if they'll let us do some?"

"I can ask."

I took a long time going home that day, walking up and down all the streets in my neighborhood, really looking at them for the first time. Not that I didn't know them, the alleys, the fences, the lanes, who lived where. But this time I was looking in a different way—where was the best place to see someone coming, which houses had the highest steps, which gave a better view but took longer to get down?

And I took so long getting home that when I walked in, everyone was already seated at the table. My father. My mother. Uncle Frans.

8

"Go wash your hands and come right to the table," my mother said.

I was glad of those extra few seconds. I had gotten so used to worrying about confronting Uncle Frans at the door that I never imagined he might already be inside when I got home.

I splashed cold water on my face and went over what I'd noticed coming in. Uncle Frans hadn't said anything yet, my mother was only impatient because I'd gotten home late. And among themselves the grown-ups did not seem upset, it was more like a little festive occasion. My mother had put her best teapot and cups out. The good plates.

I took my place at the table between my father and mother, right across from Uncle Frans. I wished everyone a polite good evening. My mother put food on my plate—good bread, smoked Gouda, a thin slice of ham and a thick slice of tomato. As I started eating, she poured tea in my cup and pushed over the sugar, full to the top as it hadn't been for a long time.

"Your Uncle Frans brought us all this food as a present," said my mother, smiling at her brother.

"Yes," said Frans, "I've been so busy I've neglected my duties to my sister. To my brother-in-law. And to my nephew."

The food went tasteless in my mouth. He may have been there for more than one reason, but one of them was me.

"It's the nicest ham I've tasted since the war started," said my father, by way of a neutral compliment.

"The NSB does important work and we're well fed for it."

"That I can see," said my mother. "Frans, I'll bet you've gained three kilos."

She was right. Frans had the same blond hair as my mother but it was thinning, and that, plus his prominent Adam's apple, had always made him look skinnier than he was. Now it was my mother who looked thin, a green vein at her temple. Uncle Frans looked sleek and we looked shabby.

My mother was happy to eat good food for the treat of it and because it would give her strength for managing with the twins and the house. My father wasn't saying anything, not wanting to spoil her happiness, especially since it had not been him who'd brought the food.

Uncle Frans didn't seem to like my father's silence. "I know what people say," said Uncle Frans. "They say the good Dutch don't join the NSB. Isn't that right, sister?"

"Yes, I've heard that," my mother said cautiously, not liking political discussions.

"People say a lot of things," continued Uncle Frans. "And

some of them are plain wrong. It's wrong to say the good Dutch don't join the NSB. I'm good Dutch, wouldn't you say?" he asked my mother and father, who both nodded. "And I see who the other NSB people are, and they're good Dutch too."

"Not all of them," said my father. He was going to allow himself that.

"No group's a hundred percent, not even a family," said Uncle Frans with a quick glance at me.

"I don't know what's going on anymore, Frans," said my mother, her voice almost tearful.

"Don't worry, it's all simple and clear."

"Tell me then," she said, turning to him.

"The Germans are on a crusade to build a new world for people like us. A world without Communists and Jews. A world where the better people live better. Who can defeat them? England? Too small. Russia? They won't die for Stalin. America? If they come in, they'll come late. Hitler brought Germany out of poverty and defeat. But you know what drew me to National Socialism more than anything else? The songs. I have never been happier in my life than when I'm standing in a square with hundreds of other people singing the same song, feeling the same thing."

I saw some relief coming into my mother's face as he made things clearer for her. But I didn't want her believing everything he said. I couldn't say anything but my father could.

He was still holding his tongue but finally spoke up. "That all may be true, Frans, but I'll tell you one thing—it's a very bad war and it's going to end very badly, even worse if you're on the losing side."

"So then what, avoid choosing sides?"

"Why not? Holland was neutral in the First War."

"Too late this time. Like it or not, we're in. Neutrality's not a choice."

"Maybe not for the country," said my father, "but it is for me."

My mother shifted in her chair and gave my father a look that meant, Don't spoil the occasion with politics.

"I'll tell you why a person can't be neutral," said Uncle Frans. "Because you've got to make choices if you want to feed your family."

He'd touched on the sore spot. My father drew back in his chair. "We haven't starved yet."

"No, not yet, but it's going to be a long war and, you're right, things will get worse before they get better. I'm not saying everyone should join the NSB. I'm saying the least people can do is listen to our ideas, as my sister was just kind enough to do."

He smiled at her and she smiled back.

At that moment she was more his sister than she was my mother or my father's wife.

My father didn't say anything. I wanted him to say something, anything, to change the feeling at the table, as long as it didn't turn the subject around to me.

"So, the first step," said Uncle Frans, who now sounded like he was lecturing, "is to listen. The second is to think it over. And the third is to show support. And, who knows, if some real feeling arises, then and only then should a person think of joining."

"Most of those who are joining," said my father, "aren't joining like that. They're in for the ham and to hell with tomorrow."

"But you ate the ham too," said Frans.

And there was nothing my father could say to that.

Then to my horror I saw what Uncle Frans was doing. By

pleasing my mother, shaming my father, he was bringing my parents under his power so they'd be weaker in defense of me.

Even though I did not feel like eating I stuffed my mouth with food so that I wouldn't be able to answer right away if Frans asked me a question and would get an extra few seconds to think. I took a long sip of tea to make the food easier to chew.

"And you know," said Frans, as if the idea were just coming into his mind as he was stirring sugar into his tea, "you know, the question of neutrality not only applies to us, it even applies to the children, at least to the boys who are getting bigger now." He gave me a look but I couldn't meet his glance.

It was coming now. It was all going to come crashing down on my head.

"What does it have to do with boys?" asked my mother, who was addressing all her questions to her brother now.

"Boys are stupid and like adventure."

"And so are some men," said my father, and Frans came to a halt to decide just what he had meant by that.

"Yes," Frans said, seeming to agree, "some are. But as I was saying, boys, some boys, are stupid and like adventure."

Now my parents knew that he meant me and I could feel their attention move toward me. My mother even gave me a quick worried look. I'd come home late, who knew what I'd been doing out there in the middle of a war? And if she knew what I had in fact been doing, she'd like it even less. But I still thought my father wouldn't mind so much. When my mother had told him I'd hidden the copper bowl in the potting shed, all he had said was, "Maybe I can find a better place."

"Some boys might even be stupid enough to try to sabotage

some German military vehicles. . . ." I could hear my mother gasp and feel my father's gloom thicken. "And now let me tell you just how stupid those boys can be. They don't know what they're doing and so they can't succeed. All they can do is get caught. And once they're caught they're in for it good, and so are the parents who let their boy go off in that direction, maybe, who knows, even gave him their blessing.

"But some stupid boys are luckier than others. At least the first time. *If* they get caught by their uncle, who gives them a good kick in the ass, which, if you want my opinion, should be repeated at home with a strap until there's nothing stupid left in that stupid boy!"

No maybes about it, my father would beat me for being stupid and for putting the family in danger, but part of him would like it that I had tried to do something against the bastards. And I'd take the beating. But what I needed now was one word from my father, a signal to me, and to Frans, that I mattered, that he'd beat me because that was the right thing for him and for me, not because anyone could tell him what to do.

But no words came to my father's lips, which had just eaten NSB bread. And my mother was now too alarmed even to speak. And Frans seemed willing to keep the silence going for as long as it took.

The air was like slowly cracking glass. I didn't think I could take it for another second.

And then I was saved by the most unlikely source—the twins.

They started crying in the next room and my mother jumped up to go to them.

Frans pulled his chair a little back from the table, making room for her to pass.

Nothing was said in the few seconds she was gone. Frans turned to watch her go, my father shot me a look of anger, then looked down at the table, and, as for me, I didn't know where to look.

And when my mother was back at the table with a twin in each arm, she said with a touch of reproach, "It must have been all the talking woke them up."

No harsh words would be spoken now with the babies at the table unless things really slipped out of hand.

"And how are my other two nephews doing?" Frans said to my mother.

"All right, but I worry about them. Soap is hard to come by, everything's just getting grimier and grimier, I worry about disease. If they were getting enough to eat, that would be one thing, but . . ."

"Sometimes extra milk comes my way," said Frans.

"I would so appreciate it. They're not growing as fast as this one did," she said with a half-glance at me. I didn't like being called "this one."

By then the twins had quieted back down.

"Let their uncle hold them for a minute," said Frans, making a gallantry of it. "I'm sure you get to hold them enough."

She smiled and very slowly and very carefully handed them over to him. They started fussing a little but Frans started singing, "Hoppy boys, hoppy boys," and rocked them up and down as if they were all on a horse.

They liked it, they liked their uncle. One way or the other, he had us all now.

Then, looking from my mother to my father, he said in a soft, pleasant voice, "What nice, smart-looking boys."

Not like me, who hadn't been dealt with yet. The twins were smiling as if happy that I was in trouble.

Then my father finally spoke to me but only to let me know just how severe the beating would be: "Go to bed and no school tomorrow."

My mother only added, "Say good night."

I rose from the table so quickly I couldn't tell what sent my teacup flying through the air, my shirtsleeve or—the twins!

9

Some words hurt even worse than the belt. But then after a
while they were both too much for me and I couldn't keep
from weeping.

That didn't mean the end of the beating, though.

"Weep now so you don't weep for worse later!"

It was only right that I was being punished for doing something so stupid and dangerous. Now I would learn my lesson
and never put my family in such danger again. This was what a
good father did to a bad son, and it did not matter that it hurt so
bad, what mattered was that we were together in this as father
and son, that was the good of it.

The blows were all different. The first ones were more startling than painful, then I was more aware of the humiliation,
pants at my ankles, ass in the air, but when the tempo suddenly

picked up, all that I knew was his unrelenting anger, a fury that only grew as it was vented. There were times when his pace slackened and I couldn't help hoping it would be over soon. But then something in the way I stood or moved told him I was getting my hopes up and he'd pick up the pace to beat the last of the stupid hope out of me.

"Don't you think I'm taking pity on you, boy, it was only my arm getting tired. And you didn't take any pity on me, did you, boy, when you went off to fight the German Army. What I'm doing to you now is nothing compared to what they would have done to me if you hadn't had the dumb luck to be caught by your uncle. They'd have strung me up by my thumbs, but you didn't think of that, did you, shit for brains!"

Then it started up again ever worse. Like we were part of a furious machine that ran on anger, that drove a belt to produce pain. Anger, leather, pain. Anger, leather, pain. Fury turned his curses into hisses and pain turned my pleas into howls. The blows were landing on open welts now, no unmarked flesh left to cushion the pain.

Then he said the words that hurt more than the belt and whose pain outlasted the welts. "No son of mine would be so stupid! No son of mine would be so stupid to risk his family's life for a brainless prank! No son of mine would put me at the mercy of that son of a bitch brother-in-law of mine! Now I see why God gave me twin boys, because you're no son of mine! No fucking son of mine!"

The next morning when I woke up in my bed, everything gave me pain, the sheets, the air, any movement. I didn't know if I was allowed to come down for food. I could smell breakfast from the kitchen. I could hear the twins making their noises.

My father was complaining about the ersatz coffee: "It tastes like shoe polish!"

"How do you know?" said my mother. "Ever try it?"

"I may soon enough."

It felt like I had died and the family was going on without me. I saw what ghosts see. That nobody misses you that much, that nobody cares that much.

A door slammed downstairs.

"Come down and eat now, Joop," my mother called from the foot of the stairs.

Getting dressed was hard, the stairs were worse. The twins were gleeful, excited by the funny way I walked to the table and the grimace on my face. The table had been cleared except for my father's bottle of Niemeijer Koffie Surrogaat. For me there was a piece of bread on a plate and a cup of tea.

I ate slowly. I wanted to make breakfast last as long as possible because I didn't know what was coming next. My father was nowhere in sight.

I could hear the twins from behind. A lot of people couldn't tell them apart. But I could. They even looked a little different if you looked close enough. But grown-ups never look as close as kids. And the twins were different by nature too. Jan was merrier, Willem, more serious.

My father came in from out back. I looked up at him. It must have been the wrong look.

"So he's eating bread and drinking tea already. I must not have taught my lesson well enough. Get up!"

I was on my feet quick since I was only sitting half on my chair anyway.

"Cellar stairs!"

He walked down the stairs behind me, watching how I walked—all trembly and meek or with a little spirit. I tried to put some spirit in it so he would be proud of me, proud at least of the way I took a licking, at least his son in that.

The cellar was dark and dank with a smell like piss and potatoes.

As I unhitched my own belt I was already being torn up inside. I wanted to do everything in the best possible way so that he would say, "I guess I was wrong, you're good and you're brave, you must be my son." But another part of me that only cared for itself just wanted no more pain, no more welts upon welts, that part didn't care if he dropped dead and would have even been glad of it. I couldn't let that part live in me at all because then he would be right and I'd be no son of his.

Still, I hoped he'd have mercy when he saw my bare ass all crisscrossed. He had none. The first three blows started right out at the maximum, no buildup, no getting used to it. All I cared about was not crying too soon.

Then the doorbell rang and the house went silent. A blow already started landed halfheartedly.

A minute later we both heard my mother's voice from the top of the stairs trying to sound calm: "NSB house search for copper."

He shot me a look but I didn't know what it meant. Was it that we were connected by the copper bowl I had hidden and he had then rehidden or was he reminding me that nothing connected us? "You don't move," he said, taking the stairs quickly.

I heard my father give his name and say, yes, he resided in that dwelling, and, no, that he had no copper to turn in.

I could hear the fear in his voice, and the anger, and I hoped that the NSB men couldn't hear it.

"Go ahead, search the place if you want," said my father. "But don't wreck it. This is a house of good Dutch."

Something was said back to him quick and sharp but I couldn't make it out through the floorboards. Boots started moving across the floor and up the stairs; there must have been four or five NSB, maybe even six.

"What's downstairs?" asked the voice that asked the questions.

"Nothing," said my father. "A root cellar. Junk. A boy being punished."

He didn't say "our son" or "*my* son."

I jumped away and pulled up my pants as the cellar door was opened wide, letting a shaft of light down the stairs. The NSB man who came down was quite tall and seemed more interested in not banging his head than in anything else. He shone his flashlight slowly around the cellar, walking over to kick a few sacks or pull some old junk away from the wall to see if there was anything behind it.

When he shone the flashlight directly at me, I could barely see him.

"You being punished?" he asked, even putting a little softness in his voice as if he cared.

I nodded.

"Tell me where their copper is," he said.

He didn't think I was their son either, otherwise he wouldn't have said it like that.

Emphasizing the first word, I said, "We got no copper."

He held the light in my eyes for another few seconds, then

shone it behind me before going back up the stairs, bent low and taking long steps.

A few minutes after the NSB had left, my father closed the cellar almost shut. I was glad, it was better than another beating.

I could sit down; the floor was cool, even soothing. I closed my eyes to make it dark because my eyes were closed, not because I was in a lightless cellar.

I even almost laughed. It was all so crazy, the war, everything—a Dutch Nazi *razzia* had just saved my poor ass.

10

I walked into the bedroom where my mother was breast-feeding both twins, all pink and naked. My heart sank when I saw little NSB armbands on both of them. She cried out when she saw me and the twins turned toward me, two tiny Uncle Franses glaring at me with anger and hatred. Suddenly their little dickies grew large and crossed like swords at a military wedding.

I woke up on the cellar floor. My bones were cold and it felt like there were cobwebs in my ears and nostrils. I knew I had slept there for hours even before I saw the late afternoon light coming from the cellar door. And I also knew the house was empty. An empty house has its own sound.

First, I was afraid that my family had snuck off to live somewhere else and left me like a cat tossed out to the street. Then I realized that couldn't be and what might have happened was even worse. The leaders of the *razzia* hadn't liked my father's answers and hadn't liked not finding our copper, and so they had dragged them all off to one of those places where they tortured people.

I stood up.

I didn't know what to do. I didn't know what I should do, could do, was allowed to do, was supposed to do, what would make my father angrier, what would start to bring back his love. I was paralyzed by fear, indecision, silence.

The only thing I was certain of was that I was hungry. Hunger moved my feet toward the stairs and put my hand on the rail. It couldn't be wrong to be hungry. Even the Queen wakes up hungry. But the Queen had fled to England, she wasn't perfect either.

I took the stairs slowly. I was afraid of what I'd see at the top. The house all a wreck, blood on the floor. But everything was just as clean and neat as always, it was just that everything seemed too still without people in it. You could almost hear the sunlight pinging off the pans hanging in the kitchen. And the blue and white dishrag on the counter looked like it was made of some kind of porcelain; I had to reach out and touch it to make sure it was real.

My cup of tea and my piece of bread were still on the table. Since my mother hadn't cleaned them away, they were still mine to have. That meant that she still cared about me but could only show it in quiet ways my father wouldn't notice.

The bread was hard and the tea was flat but as my father always said, hunger is the best sauce. I dipped the bread in the tea and when the last crust was gone I wet my finger to pick up the crumbs from the plate. I could see three green apples in a white enamel bowl on a small oak table but I couldn't allow myself even to think about taking one. What I had to decide was what to do with my cup and plate. Should I take them to the sink or leave them on the table? If I left them on the table my father might say, "Now we're supposed to wait on him!" But if I brought them to the sink, he might say, "Thinks he's one of the family again, just like that!"

I washed the plate and cup in the sink but I didn't dry them. I was afraid to use the towel but I did put my cup upside down on the plate as my mother had taught me so that she would see that I remembered.

But I didn't know what to do next. Going outside was just asking for another beating. But could I go up to my room and study for school? My father wouldn't buy that, say it was just a trick, just pretending to be a good boy, and that he hated more than anything. I needed to do the right thing, the thing that wouldn't make him angry at me, the thing that might even make him take pity on me.

If I just sat still at the table and waited for them to come home, that wouldn't be right, to just sit there and do nothing while they might be in danger. But if I tried to do some work in the house, I might do it wrong and make things worse for me. My brain was almost hurting from that much thinking.

Then I got an idea—pray to God.

"Dear God, you can see into every house so you know how much trouble I'm in and that I'm just standing here with no idea what I should do next to keep my father from getting angry with me, that's one thing, and to start getting him to love me again, that's another.

"You're our Father who art in heaven and so you know better than anyone what I should do so that my own father will love me again."

For a very long minute there was nothing, just the silence of an empty house, and I told myself, Of course there's no God; if there was, he wouldn't have let the Germans invade our country, and even if there was a God, why would he be interested in some stupid boy and his troubles, he's like a general, he can't care about every soldier that falls on the field.

But then the strangest thing happened. I can't say that God spoke to me or anything like that, there wasn't any voice, any words. But all of a sudden I did know just what to do, and I knew it had to be from God because it was the one thing I would have never thought of myself, the one thing I would never have wanted to do—go back down to the cellar. Because it was dark and cold down there and I might fall asleep again and have nightmares again, it would be a test of how much I wanted to be a part of the family again, to be my father's son again. I knew this was true and right but it was hard to make my body do it. My knees did not want to bend, my feet could not rise off the floor.

The cellar door had a white enamel knob with a web of fine cracks; it was a little loose and sometimes needed jiggling. My hand was on it but my wrist did not want to turn it. It is almost impossible to put yourself in jail but that's what I was doing, that's the way I'd been shown.

Even worse than opening the door was closing it behind me. The door swept the light away like a broom. I left it open a crack so I wouldn't fall down the stairs. I thought about going down the stairs backward like a sailor but decided there was enough light to see. Slowly, carefully, I descended the stairs until suddenly I had that funny feeling when you think there's one more step and there isn't.

I sat down with my back against a support. I kept my eyes on the sliver of light by the door. I did not want to fall asleep again. I was afraid the same nightmares would be waiting for me.

They were. The difference between sitting in the dark and looking at a sliver of light and dreaming that you were sitting in the dark and looking at a sliver of light was so small you could slip right into sleep before you knew it. A witch looked in from upstairs and saw me, cackling, "There's a bad boy down here, put on water, we'll cook him!" That woke me up, but for how long, an hour, a minute?

Then I was saved by my father, who flung open the door and yelled, "Get up here and help."

11

"Got his ass beat, got his ass beat!" the boys chanted as I walked stiff-legged across the playground.

That was still from the first beating; my father never started the second one back up again after it was interrupted by the *razzia*. Maybe that was because I gave him good help when he called me up from the cellar.

My father, mother, and the twins had left the house to go to a neighbor's who'd gotten a load of firewood and eggs. My father bought some and then it had to be brought in quick from the street. And maybe because I was trying to show him that I was worth something, I didn't feel much pain and my legs worked better than that first Monday back at school, the boys chanting and taunting.

I walked right through them; they let me pass, though one of them took a slap at my ass, making all the rest laugh. Made bold by his example, a little kid tried the same thing but wasn't quick enough and my knuckles caught his nose just right. Now the boys yelled at me for hitting a little kid but I didn't care. I stopped and turned to show them I was ready to fight, that I wasn't afraid of them.

And I wasn't afraid of them because all my fear was reserved for meeting Kees.

In front of me I could see a few boys kicking a ball around; it was late fall, the leaves yellow—on the trees and on the ground. I looked in the far corners of the playground, moving slowly forward. I couldn't spot Kees. I felt the relief you feel when you don't have to face something right away.

But it wasn't long before I heard the boys start up their chanting again, softer and more good-humored than it'd been with me because they liked Kees better and feared his anger more.

I turned and saw him coming, walking like I walked.

The boys could see that he was heading for me, that we had something to talk about, two of a kind.

As soon as he was beside me, I started moving again. I didn't want anyone to hear any part of our talk. After a few steps, he said, "You told."

I couldn't say anything. That meant I admitted it. I could not deny it, it was so obviously true. Frans had been to their house, told Kees's parents everything, maybe even asked to see Kees. So he could then make an identification like a proper policeman.

I hoped that would be enough.

I hoped that would be everything.

Then we would be comrades of the beaten ass and the brave but failed resistance, though it's never good to be partners in any failure.

But that wasn't enough.

That wasn't everything,

Kees had to ask a question. "You told before you were beaten, or after?"

What was the difference, would either of us be walking any different?

But I couldn't ask that question because he would know what answer it contained.

"After," I said.

"Liar."

"I'm not."

"You are."

"I wouldn't have told before," I said.

"I wouldn't have told at all."

"You would've."

"They never beat you past a certain limit, they're afraid you'll end up at the doctor's and cost them a pretty penny."

But my lie was having some effect. He was off what I had done and on to what he would have done.

"You didn't have anything to tell anyone," I said.

"I didn't tell everything my father asked me."

"What was there to tell?"

"About the sand, the trucks, there were things to tell."

"My uncle would have already told him."

"Maybe."

He didn't say that "maybe" with much conviction. His anger was dying down, dampened by doubt. It looked like he was going to keep on walking with me until he thought of something else to say. And that meant we were still something like friends.

12

All I wanted was to be my father's boy again. To hear him call me son.

So I hit on the idea of knocking around the city and seeing if I couldn't make a few guilders; maybe that'd wear away the hard look in my father's eyes.

I walked from the Dam to West Church to the Pijp. The city looked pretty much the same if you didn't look too close. There was a fine layer of brown grime on everything. And what's Amsterdam without sparkling glass? People smelled sour, the canals like pissoirs.

Since I was out and around so much I saw a lot. Like when the NSB decided to show the Germans that Dutchmen could beat up Jews too. The only problem was that the Jews from the boxing club Maccabi got themselves a wagon to take them over to where the trouble was. The brawl was on at Koco, a Jewish ice cream parlor on Rijnstraat. A bunch of NSB and German police went in and started beating up Jews right at their tables. But then the Maccabi wagon pulled up and out came the boxers. Even though there were fewer of them, they had two advantages— they were fighting mad and they knew how to fight. The NSB were just fucking around and the truth was that most of them had no appetite for the real thing. So when the boxers started breaking noses with every punch, the NSB began quickly backing away over the broken glass, tripping over women on the floor.

I was glad to see the NSB get it and kept looking for Uncle Frans in the crowd, that would have been so perfect, but no such luck. When you don't want him, he's there; when you do, he isn't.

I made money any way I could. I cleaned the ice off an old lady's stairs. I helped load a van, happening by just as one mover's back went out. I put up posters. I don't remember any of them except for one I must have put up much later, after Hitler and Stalin stopped pretending to be friends. That one said, BOLSHEVISM IS MURDER. On the floor a murdered father and child, a broken crucifix, a mother screaming over them. Probably put up two hundred of them. I got used to the picture after a while, but in the beginning it got to me. What if that was us? My father and me dead on the floor, my mother out of her mind with grief. Even now when nothing really terrible had happened, she was not her usual self. Something she might have mentioned once or maybe twice, now she'd go on and on about it. Like "fine, high-quality soap."

"You can't get really fine, high-quality soap for love or

money. There's a stink in the house. Not a big one yet, not one a man could smell. But *I* can smell it, so can other women who come to visit. Even the wallpaper is starting to stink if you stand close to it. I'm even starting to stink to myself."

I worked awhile for a cobbler, searching through his scrap bin for pieces that matched, or came close. No new leather was coming in and people had to walk more, their shoes wearing out faster than usual. He told people to start wearing wooden clogs, to stuff them with hay in the wintertime to keep their feet warm, or newspaper if they couldn't get hay.

"You think it'll come to that?" asked one customer.

"That. And past that."

Some days he hated his work. "A whole life bent over a pair of old dirty shoes! That was worth being born for, having to die for?" Then he would set his tools aside, roll himself a cigarette from some ersatz shag he hated as much as my father hated ersatz coffee, pick a piece off his tongue, and say to me, "What do you think we should do to Hitler if we catch him?"

"I think everyone in Holland should get a whack at him with an ax until he's nothing but a bloody pulp."

"That's pretty good, that's pretty good," he said.

"What's your idea?"

"I want him naked in a frying pan too big to climb out of, and the hotter it gets the louder he screams."

"Good one," I said.

When I was done matching all the pieces in his bin, he patched my shoes and paid me what I had coming. Counting the coins and thinking of my mother, I asked him if he knew where any good soap could be had. He only laughed and held up his hands, black from dirty leather and shoe polish.

At first I gave the money I earned right to my father. To show him that he had beaten all the stupidity out of me. To show him that now I understood and was grateful that he had done his duty as a father. He took the money without saying a word. I could feel that he liked it that I was out earning money but thought it too soon to say anything to me.

One day when I was handing him the money, he said, "From now on, give it . . ." I knew he was about to say "to your mother" but then on the spot he decided he didn't want me doing that either. He was the one to give her money, not me.

From a high shelf in the kitchen he got down the Bensdorp cocoa tin, which had been empty for a long time now but still smelled of cocoa when he opened it, reminding me of winter days before the war.

"You get money, it goes in here," he said, saying not one word more than he had to.

Still, it was a good idea. I liked the clang of the coins and the smell of cocoa, fainter each time I lifted the lid.

It was the usual lousy Dutch winter with sleet blowing in from the North Sea. There was a lot of excitement in late February when the whole city and most of the country went on a protest strike after the Germans picked up four hundred Jews in a big raid. Dutch people were also worried about being sent to Germany to do forced labor. It was great knocking about Amsterdam those couple of days, everyone out and excited, but then the Germans started executing people and everyone went back to work.

Winter was better for earning money than spring. In winter things were always freezing and busting, you could always turn a few pennies off it. What I brought home never came to much but sometimes when I gave the cocoa can a shake it made a good, encouraging sound, a lot of coins against metal. And sometimes I'd notice there wouldn't be many of them at all in there, meaning that they'd gotten used, also a good feeling. Either way it didn't seem to affect my father much. He spoke to me a little more often, but only to tell me what needed doing, never to praise or just talk. He rarely called me by name, never called me son.

What was good about the spring was watching the air war at night. I could feel the British bombers coming long before I could see or hear them. Plates would start rattling in the cupboard, the floorboards would hum. I'd go up to the roof.

The searchlights pecked around the clouds for British planes on their way to bomb Germany. Sometimes the searchlights would crisscross and trap a tiny buzzing insect of a plane. The *ack-ack* guns sounded even more excited when they actually had something in their sights. If you were lucky you'd see them get a plane, which went down like a shooting star.

One hot night in late June I sat for an hour hoping to see a plane go down in flames, not because I was against the British but because it was just more interesting when that happened. When the guns fell silent I went back downstairs to get some water.

Frans was at the table with my mother and father. My father looked alarmed when he saw me. The look only lasted for a second but I saw it. I didn't understand it, though. I was the one who was supposed to be afraid of him, not the other way around.

And when Uncle Frans turned in my direction, his eyes had none of their usual searching disapproval. Maybe it was the peppermint schnapps they were all drinking, but Frans looked merry, even happy. My mother was always in a good mood when her brother came over, not only because he never came empty-handed but because they made each other younger by remembering their childhood.

"You loved your tin soldiers even back then," she said to him. "Didn't you keep them in a cigar box?"

"Until they all smelled like Havana cigars," said Frans, smiling and half closing his eyes.

"So I can see why you like to put different-colored pins on your map, especially now that the Germans have invaded Russia," she said.

"I'll be moving more than pins," said Frans.

"Meaning?"

"Meaning that NSB members in good standing have been allowed the honor of volunteering to smash the Bolsheviks in their lair."

For a second my mother didn't understand what he was talking about.

"In other words . . . ?"

"Ever since I was a boy playing with those tin soldiers, my dream has been to enter a city as a conqueror. Now I have my chance. We ship out in five days."

For a long moment no one said anything. The news was too startling. Frans was now part of the big world, the world of airplanes, armies, burning cities, and we'd be left behind in the small world of house and school, street and kitchen.

Just as my mother's shoulders began to shudder as they always did before she began crying, Frans, as if already a soldier, ordered her not to cry. "To get through these times a person must be proud and hard." He rose and walked over to her and put his hand on her shoulder. "Proud and hard."

Still standing, Frans picked up the bottle of peppermint schnapps and refilled all their glasses. My mother wiped away her tears on her sleeve and looked up at him, her eyes shining with admiration. My father kept his eyes on his glass.

"I would propose a toast," said Frans, looking off into the far distance, which only he could see. He motioned for me to approach the table and even poured a few drops into my water glass, which was now empty. "I would propose a toast to the health of Adolf Hitler, who has created a heroic epoch in which dreams come true."

We all raised our glasses to Hitler and dreams.

13

The war took the place of the Olympics for us kids. Especially after Russia and America were in. The armies were teams, the battles were matches.

In the schoolyard we argued about who was going to win all the time, a dozen kids talking all at once.

"How can Germany beat America and Russia? It's like a tiger attacking two elephants."

"It doesn't matter how big a country is. A hundred bombers can destroy a whole city, like the Germans did to Rotterdam."

"The bastards killed my aunt and two cousins there."

"But we better hope the Germans win because otherwise the Russians will come and take everything away from our parents and put us in dormitories where everybody sleeps under one huge blanket."

"No, what'll happen is first, the Americans will beat the Germans, then turn around and whip the Russians."

"But what if the Germans don't lose? What if they beat Russia quick then hit the Americans so hard they decide it's not worth it and go back to their skyscrapers? Then the kids' parents who were smart enough to join the NSB will be the ones with everything."

"But if the Germans do lose, those parents will get an ax in the head."

"Like Joop's flickin' Uncle Frans," said Kees.

"I hate him too! I'll take an ax to him," I said, but the damage was already done. It was never good for anyone to know you had NSB in the family. It's not your fault, they'd say, what someone in your family does, but what they really meant was the apple never falls far from the tree. What they really meant was that never happened with the true, good Dutch.

After that some of the kids who palled around with me always found a good reason not to play with me, their eyes were always looking elsewhere when I was around. Worse, some of the other kids who had NSB in the family tried to get chummy with me, birds of a feather, strength in numbers. But I shunned them as I was shunned.

The net result was that I was more alone than ever, which had one advantage—it gave me more time to prowl the city in search of high-quality soap and money. Some of the other boys heard that I was getting good at shaking money from the streets and wanted to come with me and learn my tricks. If you've got money you've got friends, and if you can show people how to get money you've got friends too. I took on a few boys as partners and taught them some of what I'd learned. We'd stand on street corners watching people go by, trying to guess who was richer than he looked and who was poorer than he dressed. I showed them where to wait for people lugging heavy bundles, where the streets were steepest, slipperiest. I taught them how to gauge what a job might fetch and always to ask a little less.

Mostly, though, it wasn't a good arrangement. The kids who weren't good workers held me back while the good ones soon went off for themselves and became the competition. Either way I lost money. Sometimes my father would shake the cocoa can and glower at me when the sound of the coins was measly and thin. Not that he ever said anything good when the can jangled good.

Everything was getting thin. The soles on my shoes. The lining of my jacket. Even the heat in the house seemed thin, not much warmer than the outside air. I went back to the cobbler to see if I could do some more work for him in exchange for some shoe repair, but his shop was all boarded up. Either he was a Jew or just out of business. Jews were being barred from more and more activities and professions. They couldn't go to cafés, museums, theaters, even zoos. It made my father furious. He said to my mother, "I got the worst goddamed luck in the world! You know what a Jew is to me? A stomach with two legs and a wallet. A customer. And there's less of them all the time."

My mother did not seem to be as interested in his complaints or as amused by his choice of words as she once would have been. She looked up from reading one of Frans's letters, which came about once a month from Russia and were addressed to the whole family but were really only to her. "Frans writes," she said, " 'I'll never complain about Dutch winters again.' "

"So your brother hasn't entered any cities as a conqueror yet."

"How do you know? I haven't finished his letter yet."

"No Soviet cities have fallen to the Germans yet but Kiev, and he wouldn't be complaining of the winter there."

"How do you know all that?"

"I've been listening to broadcasts from England."

"So now it's you who's putting the family in danger," she said, turning abruptly back to the letter.

Sharp as they were, I liked her words, which put me and my father together since listening to Dutch broadcasts from London was strictly forbidden.

You twins didn't like it when our mother spoke sharply. You would freeze at whatever you were doing and exchange looks. You were hers entirely. You loved our father too, of course, and were happy when he played with you on the floor with my old wooden trucks, there being no money for new toys, not that there were any around. My father found a little dark blue paint out in the back shed and now, instead of many different faded colors, my old trucks and cars were all dark blue.

You twins looked more like our mother, slender and blond, than like my father and me, stocky with bristly, reddish brown hair. You both even had the same green vein at the side of your forehead as she had. Sometimes when my father came home in the evening she would say, "The boys weren't feeling well today," and I'd be right there wanting to yell, I'm one of your boys too, and I feel fine today, but somehow the words could never make it from my mind to my mouth.

My mother was always worried about you twins' health because you were more delicate and because the things that kept you healthy—food, heat, cleanliness—were in shorter supply with each passing day. We weren't burning the furniture in the woodstove or eating tulip bulbs for dinner yet, but those days no longer seemed so far in the future.

My mother wasn't talking about soap as much as before but she was constantly checking her fingernails for dirt or turning her head to the side like a bird to smell herself. Except to shop and walk you twins, she never went out. What I hated most was when she asked me to take you two to the park and watch you as you played. I was always afraid you'd hurt yourselves and I'd get the blame. I was afraid I'd do something to you without meaning to, like turning away just as you were falling. I didn't even like taking your hands to cross a street. You can always tell if someone likes you by his hand. Your hands didn't like me at all.

14

Just as all the yellow flowers, the crocus, the forsythia, were coming out in '42, the Jews had to start wearing yellow stars with the word JOOD written on them in letters that were supposed to look like Hebrew. To add insult to injury, the Jews had to pay for the stars, four cents apiece. And supply was limited, only four to a customer.

Since I was always out and around the city I heard what people said about the yellow stars. At first there was some outrage and a lot of talk about everyone wearing yellow stars so the Germans wouldn't know who was who. But it was all talk. No one was that brave. Or that stupid.

People had all sorts of reactions to seeing who was wearing the stars. Surprise. Shock. Disappointment. Anger. Some people felt that they'd been deceived by people they hadn't known were Jewish.

"You'd think they'd have mentioned it. But no, they hid it. You can't trust people who hide things like that. What else are they hiding?"

But some people made a point of greeting their Jewish friends on the street until they noticed that this made them feel even more singled out.

It was worst in mixed marriages where, say, the father had to wear the star but the mother and children did not.

I had a problem with the stars too, but not like the Jews. My problem was that you twins loved the stars and wanted me to get stars for you too.

"We want yellow stars, we want yellow stars," you'd say at the same time.

"You can't have them, you're not Jews."

"Yes, we are, we're twins and we're Jews."

"No, we're Protestants."

"We want stars, we want yellow stars."

One day when I was with you two in the park I saw one of our teachers walking by quickly, smoking his pipe. Even though he was only a math teacher, I asked him if he could explain to you two why you couldn't wear stars. He squatted down, still puffing on his pipe.

"You can't wear stars," he said.

"Why not?"

"Because you're not Jews."

"What are Jews?"

"Jews are people who don't believe Jesus Christ is the Son of God."

"Who do the Jews think Jesus is?" I asked.

"To them he's just another Jew."

"Why? Is he?"

"Well, his mother and father were Jews."

"The Germans say if your mother and father are Jews then you're a Jew too," I said.

"Yes, they do."

"So, if Jesus was here, he'd have to wear a yellow star too?" I asked.

"You know, I guess he would," said the math teacher, rising back up.

As I watched him walk away down the gravel path I was more confused than ever.

"We want yellow stars, we want yellow stars!" you two yelled with one voice.

"All right, all right," I said. "Next time, you'll have them."

You and Jan were happy and excited when I brought you home, which made our mother smile as she sliced us some green apple.

Later that evening as I went off to bed I saw my mother talking to my father and I knew she was talking about me. He looked up at me, not with love yet, but with interest, new eyes.

I made two little stars from an old yellow napkin and wrote the word JOOD with black ink from school. I made you both promise never to mention them to anyone, ever, and not to ask to wear them until we were at the far end of the park. I don't know why the yellow stars made you two so happy. I could feel your little ribs under their shirts as I pinned on the stars. You almost stood at attention. As far as I could tell, the yellow stars didn't play any special part in your games. It was enough just to have them on.

The happier you two were, the more nervous I got. I imagined all sorts of calamities. An NSB man in a black uniform with red epaulettes would see us playing and ask if these twins were my brothers. I'd say yes then he'd ask where my star was. I'd say I lost mine and he'd say, "Let's go to your house, I'll tell your parents where they can buy one." Or if I told him the truth and said that the twins were only pretending to be Jews, he'd roar, "Pretending to be Jews! That's even worse than being one. I'll show you what happens to pretend Jews!"

By that summer Jews were already being called up and sent to Germany and Poland. To do forced labor. To be worked to death like old horses, some people said. By that summer Jews were already going into hiding, "diving under," that was the expression. Sometimes you'd see a whole family wearing five layers of clothing on a warm July day and you'd know they were going into hiding and try not to look at them.

I was scared Kees might come by and see you two. He'd say, "What a family, NSB uncles, squealer sons, and pretend Jews; why don't you people just try being plain good Dutch for a change? But that'd just be a waste of time. You can't be what you just aren't."

But even though Kees lived close to the park, I never saw him once.

I was even afraid of the Jews. I was afraid that some of the tough Jews, the boxers who broke Nazi noses at the ice cream parlor, would be passing by the park and know just by looking that the stars weren't real and think we were making fun of them and start punching me with fists hard as radiators.

But that didn't happen either. Nothing I worried about happened, and what happened was something I could never have foreseen.

At first I barely noticed the two of them. I only paid attention to people who could get me into trouble and that wasn't them. And they had no interest in me or you two. They were usually hugging and kissing as if they were home with the curtains drawn. Sometimes they would snap out of it and look fearfully around to see if anyone was watching. Sometimes they argued and I could hear their voices without being able to make out what they were saying. They didn't seem to be speaking Dutch. After they argued she would cry and he would take her in his arms again, though once he did slap her.

She always wore the same light blue dress and hat. Her hair was long and brown and looked as if it had just been brushed. He was stocky, with a gypsy mustache, and his dark blue suit was a little too big, he was always pushing the sleeves back up onto his forearms. He smoked a lot. They both wore yellow stars, which they tried to hide because Jews weren't allowed in parks. He'd take off his jacket, she'd put on a light sweater.

That day when I got to our part of the park and reached in my pocket for the stars, I only found one. I had been in such a hurry when we left that I had forgotten to check to see if I had both. If one had fallen out between the house and the park, that was all right, I could make another one, but if it had fallen out in the house there'd be trouble. I tried to think of a story to tell my mother about it but it was hard to think because you two were already squealing, "We want our stars, we want our stars!"

"There's only one star today, you've got to take turns."

"Me first," said Jan.

"No, me first," said you, Willem.

"If you fight about it, neither of you'll get to wear it."

That made you two quiet. "Whoever wears it second gets to wear it longer." You both thought about that for a moment, then almost at the same instant said, "Me first."

I had a coin in my pocket, one of those Nazi Dutch coins with the tulip on it that everyone hated.

"All right," I said, putting the star on the ground. "We're going to flip a coin. Who wants the tulip side?"

"I do!" you both cried.

"You can't both have the tulip."

"Willem can have the tulip," said Jan. "I'll take the star." He grabbed it from the ground and started running off.

Willem, you immediately burst into tears. I couldn't leave you like that. "Stay right here and you'll have the star first, all right?"

"All right."

"Remember, don't move."

Then I took off after Jan, who was running toward the couple on the bench, holding the star out in front of him, to say, Can you help me on with this, please?

I got there just as he was handing the star to the woman.

"Is this your brother?" the woman said to me in German.

"Yes, he is my bother," I answered in German.

"He should have his star on all the time. And so should the other twin. And so should you."

She was reaching forward, about to pin the star on Jan. From behind me I could hear you, Willem, starting to wail again as you watched.

"Wait," I said. "His brother gets to wear the star first. I

promised him. And anyway, they don't have to, they're not Jews."

"Not Jews?" said the woman.

"Why are they wearing stars then?" asked the man.

"They like to."

"They like to. . . ." said the woman, laughing a little then crying a little as well.

It felt strange to see them up close after seeing them so often from a distance. She was very pretty but her teeth were discolored. His eyes were bloodshot.

"So you're not a Jew either," he said.

"No."

"Do you know the city well?"

"Very well."

The man exchanged looks with the woman and they spoke for a minute in their language.

"Can you stay out after dark?"

"My parents let me. Sometimes I have little jobs."

"I have a little job for you tonight," said the man. "Not hard, won't take much time. You just take an envelope from my house to her house."

"Why don't you do it yourself?"

"Jews aren't allowed out between eight in the evening and six in the morning."

"But you come to the park and that's not allowed either."

"The penalty's less."

"Will the Germans kill me if they catch me with the envelope?"

"No, us."

"What will you pay me?"

"How much do you want?"

"I don't want money."

"What do you want?"

"A bar of soap. Fine, high-quality soap."

They said a few more words in their language. Then the man wrote his address on a piece of paper. "Come here at eight o'clock. I will tell you her address when I give you the envelope for her. When you give her the envelope, she will give you the soap."

"Fine, high-quality soap."

"Yes," he said in a voice that was suddenly very tired, "fine, high-quality."

15

I searched my room right away for the missing yellow star but didn't find it then or later. I knew that my mother hadn't come across it either because she would have said something as soon as I came back from the park with you twins, but she only looked at us with a faint smile and went back to her work. When I told her I'd be going out that night because I had a chance to make a little money, she only nodded.

Just as I was about to leave the house that night and was passing the shelf where my mother kept Frans's letters next to some dried flowers and a seashell, I heard the sound of distant gunfire and had the strong feeling that I should take one of those letters with me. My mother wasn't looking. I didn't even hesitate a second.

The door clicked shut behind me. It was a nice enough evening, some blue left in the sky, some warmth left in the air. A few people were out strolling. Soldiers were singing in the bar across the canal. I went the other way.

I wasn't scared yet, or not very. I hadn't done anything yet. Still, I didn't want to walk past those soldiers. What if they called me over and wanted to be friendly? The younger soldiers had been sent off to battle now and been replaced by older men who missed their own sons.

It used to be that Amsterdamers were proud to have passersby look into their houses and always kept their big front windows sparkling clean and the drapes pulled back, to say, Look in, see how nice we live. But all windows were now covered with blackout paper and some front windows were boarded up or taped up because people were afraid of the flying glass in case a bomb fell nearby or a British plane crashed, which practically never happened. People weren't proud of their houses and the lives they were leading in them anymore, and so the houses seemed to be turning away from the street.

I'd taken a minute to plan out my route but once I got going my feet knew just where to go, what alley to take, what bridge to avoid.

At one point I passed near the hotel where my father worked. More than anything I wanted him to know that his son was out in the night risking danger to get soap for his mother so she could be happy and make his father so happy he would love his son again.

The address the man had given me was one of those old houses in Amsterdam that leans against the one beside it like drunk buddies coming back from a night on the town. I knocked on the door but no one answered. I knocked again, louder. Maybe the man had been picked up and sent by train to Germany to do forced labor; that happened every day now. Or maybe he had been shot down in the street; that happened too, though not every day. Or maybe the house had been raided and he'd escaped out the back. It made me sad to think I wouldn't be getting the soap for my mother.

I was just about to knock one more time when the door opened. The man with the mustache pulled me into the darkened hallway, saying, "Good boy, you came, good." He had a pinch-the-cat, a little flashlight that worked when you squeezed its sides. He flashed it on the envelope, which was too big to fit into my pocket. I put the envelope inside my shirt, which I then tucked in tight enough to keep it in but not so tight anyone could see its outline against my shirt.

"Good," he said. "Smart boy. Now listen, I'll tell you the address."

He had trouble saying *gracht* but I understood him. "I'm not going to write the address down, you understand?" he said.

"I understand."

"Repeat the address."

"One forty-seven Keizergracht."

"Good. Good. In one second, go."

He released the pressure on the pinch-the-cat and the hallway went dark. I could feel the envelope against my skin and his tobacco-stained breath on my face. Then his hand was on my shoulder, the door was opened just enough for me to slip through. "Go," he said, "go."

Maybe it was because my eyes had just gotten used to the dark, maybe it was because I now had something dangerous inside my shirt, but somehow the city looked different. The houses seemed to turn away from me now not because they were ashamed of themselves but because they didn't want to have anything to do with me. The muscles at the backs of my legs were vibrating. But, I told myself, It isn't far. Less than ten minutes. Ten minutes at the most.

The few people I saw gave me nervous looks, knowing I couldn't be up to any good and wanting to put distance between us.

I was halfway across the bridge that led to her house when a voice from behind me said, "Stop, boy."

I stopped. But I didn't turn around, just hunched forward a little to look submissive but really to hide the envelope.

He came around in front of me. A German soldier with long creases in his face. "Where are you going?"

"Home."

"What are you doing out so late?"

"I was visiting my aunt."

"Visiting? Alone?"

"My father is working. My mother is home with the twins. But my parents wanted my aunt to see this." I pulled the letter from Uncle Frans out from my pocket. The soldier could see at once it was Germany military mail. "It's from my mother's brother. My uncle Frans. *He's* fighting the Communists. *He's* in Russland."

I don't know where I got the nerve. The soldier was taken aback for a second and said nothing. "Good luck to him then." With a little push on my shoulder he sent me on my way.

A wind had picked up. The moon kept disappearing behind clouds. I didn't look back.

The woman was waiting in the hallway wearing the same

light blue suit. She hugged me to her as if she knew me then dropped to one knee. Again I could see how pretty she was except for her teeth. I handed her the envelope, wanting to tell her the story of how the voice had prompted me to take Uncle Frans's letter and how that had saved me on the bridge, which must mean that God was watching over me and them too, but all that would have been too hard for me to say in German and it wasn't time for stories.

She opened the envelope, checking to make sure everything was there. Her face was serious, she seemed to have forgotten about me. But then a second later, with a sad smile, she handed me a small package wrapped in brown paper and tied with string. I could smell the soap's lavender scent even through the paper.

"Thank you," I said.

"No, thank you," she said.

I ran home.

My mother said, "You worked?"

"I did."

"Why aren't you putting the money in the cocoa can?"

I walked over to her and said, "Close your eyes."

The next night when my father came home from work, I heard my mother say, laughing and excited, "Smell me. Smell my skin and hair."

16

It was the winter of Stalingrad.

No more letters came from Uncle Frans. Worried that he was dead or would be soon, my mother read his last letter over and over.

For the first time my mother asked my father what he heard on his friend's radio.

"It's too soon to tell," he said. "If Germany wins the battle, Russia's cut in half. If Russia wins, Hitler's out of luck."

Sometimes I prayed to God for my mother to get a letter, just one letter, that would let her know that her brother was still alive. But sometimes, once I started asking, I'd lose all self-control. Before I knew it I'd be asking God for a motorcycle with a sidecar. My father would ride the motorcycle wearing a helmet and goggles and I'd be in the sidecar wearing a helmet and goggles too. Sometimes the sidecar would even lift into the air when we took a corner a little too fast. My father would look over to me to make sure I was all right and wink when he saw I was having the time of my life. We'd drive off deep into the countryside, where we'd trade jewelry and tobacco to farmers for potatoes, bacon, apples, milk, and cheese. At every stop my father would introduce me: "This is my son Joop." "This is my boy Joop." "This is my Joop."

One day there was a knock at the door and I had the strongest feeling that it was the postman with the letter from Uncle Frans that I had prayed for. But when I opened the door I was so surprised to see Kees that I forgot to be disappointed, especially because just as I opened the door he sneezed so hard it almost doubled him over, which made me laugh out loud, and he laughed too until he sneezed a second time, and we both laughed all the harder after that, blowing away any memory of our past troubles.

"In or out," said my mother, coming by with the twins and not wishing to lose an ounce of heat. "Don't stand there sneezing and laughing." But even she had to smile at the sight of it.

I grabbed my jacket and hat. Outside we walked a little way before he said, "I came for a special—" but that sentence ended in a sneeze, the kind that hovers at the top for a couple of seconds before finally going over.

"This stupid sneezing, it started this morning and won't stop."

"Maybe we should go indoors."

"No. Anyway, I came for a special reason. You know Maarten, who lives on your street?"

"Sure. He was the one who warned me about the *razzia* for copper."

"Right. Well now I'm warning you about him. The Ger-

mans caught him doing something, brought him in, did whatever they did, and now he's reporting to them—tells them
who's helping the resistance, who's hiding Jews."

It didn't seem possible. Marteen was handsome and the best
athlete and as good Dutch as they come.

"So, Kees, you're going around warning people?"

"Right. Want to help?"

"I do. But wait here a second, I've got to run back to my
house."

I was back in a minute with a shovel over my shoulder.

"What's that for?" he asked.

"Well, if the Germans see us going from house to house, they
might get suspicious. But this way we'll just look like a couple
of boys out trying to make money shoveling steps. Who knows,
we might even make a few guilders."

Kees looked at me with surprised admiration. I couldn't ask
for anything more.

In between warning people, we talked and laughed, old
friends glad to put their quarrel aside.

"I heard the Russians are killing the Germans real good at
Stalingrad," he said.

"You think Hitler'll surrender?"

"No, the Russians will have to drive the Germans across Europe and into the sea before that happens."

"But then the Russians'll be here!" I said.

"Can't be worse than the Germans."

We even made some money shoveling. It was late when I returned home. My parents watched me as I marched across the
living room floor to the cocoa can. It always jingled nicely to
the fall of coins but the smell was long gone now.

The next day I was up early. It wasn't a bad day. The sidewalks weren't frozen so hard you had to worry about slipping but they hadn't turned to pure slush either. The sun wasn't out but every so often the clouds would brighten. The best thing about the day was that I was getting a chance to help my father, though I didn't know at what. We were pulling a sled. On it was a canvas bag full of clanking iron tools.

On the way to wherever we were going we met De Boer, the butcher. You could see all the red veins in his nose as if a few layers of skin had been buffed off.

"Von Paulus's army is kaput," he said to my father, looking around even though there wasn't a soul in sight. I knew the general's name from other conversations about Stalingrad.

"*Kaput ist gut,*" said my father with a little smile.

"What's all this?" said De Boer with a nod at the sled.

"There's a house over on Falckstraat. I got a call last night. They cleared the Jews out. Plenty of good wood in the interior."

"Did someone tip off the police?"

"Don't know."

"If you ever need a little extra to eat, I'm working in food distribution now. Warehouse Six," said De Boer. Then he patted my shoulder. "Good boy, helping your father."

As we walked away, my father said, "Some of the wood's for us, and some's for my cousin Helen. She's sick and got no one to help her, her kids are small, and her husband's doing forced labor in Germany."

"Can I ask a question?"

He didn't answer right away. It was clear that a little conversation had started but he still hadn't decided how much closer he would allow me.

"Let's hear it."

"Will the Russians drive the Germans all across Europe and into Holland?"

"That's a good ways off yet. Ordinarily they'd stop at Berlin, but the Russians just might be so furious at being invaded that they'll want to drive the Krauts into the sea," he said.

But then I made the mistake of asking a follow-up question. "And will the Russians bring the Jews back with them?"

"No! The Jews aren't coming back!" he said angrily. "That's not our problem! Our problem is staying alive, our problem is not dying. Of hunger, of cold. If we strip the wood from an apartment, it's like . . . it's like . . . it's like you're sitting on the curb starving and along comes a man eating a steak tartare sandwich, then the police grab him and the sandwich falls to the ground; you're starving, so what do you do, sit there and wonder why the man was arrested until somebody else grabs the sandwich or some car drives over it and makes it no good for anybody? No, that's not what you do, what you do is grab the goddamned sandwich! And that's just what we're doing with the wood, you understand?"

I had made him angry, the last thing I wanted. I decided to risk a little joke. "I understand, we're just going for some steak tartare sandwiches."

"Don't I just wish it," he said, his voice suddenly soft and wistful. "Don't I just."

In the Jews' house it was colder than outside. There was still food on the table, egg and bread on a plate. Every once in a while strange smells would float by, Jew smells, anyway, smells you wouldn't smell in a Dutch house.

"The spokes on the banister'll make good kindling," said my

father, pointing at the staircase with a crowbar he was strong enough to hold straight out.

I took a hammer from the tools he'd lined up on the canvas sack. I was afraid of the house, afraid of angering him again, but all that went away as soon as I knocked out the first few spokes from the banister. Boys love breaking things, and doing it with your father and for the good of your family, what could be better. It wasn't long before I'd get angry with any spoke that resisted my hammer and I'd curse it as I slammed it all the harder. Once I looked up and caught my father grinning at my zeal.

But some of that zeal disappeared as I worked my way up the staircase and could no longer see my father in the living room prying off the woodwork with his crowbar. It would resist too, bend and bend, until it finally came cracking free.

I thought I heard something upstairs. I hammered hard at the spokes to drown out the sound. Then I stopped. All I could hear was my father puffing. Then I heard it again. Like a baby crying. Maybe the police had come and arrested the Jews so fast that they hadn't taken the baby. Or maybe they just didn't take babies; what good were they in a labor camp?

"Why'd you stop?" came my father's voice.

"I thought I heard something."

"Like what?"

"A baby."

"A baby?" He paused for a moment. "Finish the spokes."

I could hear him cursing at the reluctant wood as I went back to bashing spokes that looked like they'd burn nice. I heard wood crash to the floor downstairs but knew my father wasn't hurt because he hollered in triumph and anyway, a second later he was on the stairs, crowbar still in hand. He checked the spokes.

"Good job," he said.

Just then the sound came again from the second floor and we both heard it. He put his finger to his lips and started moving up the stairs. When he was a step or two past me, I began following him, my hammer at the ready. My father was hunched low, practically crawling up the last few stairs, then he suddenly lunged forward with the crowbar extended in front of him, which smashed open the door on the landing.

A gray cat flew out so fast it was over us and down the stairs before we even knew what had happened, then we just lay on the stairs laughing like two drunk buddies who couldn't make it home.

Back downstairs, I tied up the spokes in a bundle while my father axed a bookcase into sections that would lie flat on the sleigh.

"There's a piece of wainscoting, I couldn't get it myself, maybe the two of us together can do it," he said, handing me a smaller crowbar. When we had tapped our crowbars behind the wainscoting with our hammers, I looked over at him for the signal.

"One, two, three, all together," he said. The wainscoting creaked but did not separate much from the wall.

After a few seconds' rest, we went at it again. This time nails emerged from the wall, little clouds of plaster dust flew.

"Once more, hard, hard, together, and pull!"

And for one perfect moment we were so united that nothing could resist us and the baseboard separated so fast we almost lost our balance, which made us laugh again.

The only bad thing was that when my father was splitting up the baseboard, one of the nails punctured his finger and he started cursing a blue streak. I ran in the kitchen and grabbed him a rag.

As we were leaving I looked back and said, "They didn't have much."

"Not all Jews are rich."

On the way to his cousin Helen's, his finger started hurting again. He'd curse, unwrap his finger, suck on it.

Helen's daughter let us in. Helen was asleep on a cot by the woodstove, her face pale and sweaty. The stove was almost out, flickering, more light than heat.

"Put in some kindling," my father said to me.

The sound of the wood being moved woke up Helen. For a second or two she didn't understand what was going on. My father didn't say anything because he was busy sucking blood out of his finger.

"Is that your boy?" said Helen, looking at me.

For a second he didn't answer then said, "One of them."

The sickness came to me in my sleep. I went to bed healthy and woke up with barely enough strength to call for my mother. She knelt by the bed and put her hand on my forehead. I could tell by the fear on her face how hot I was. That made me feel bad. I wanted to bring home soap and money, not sickness. I closed my eyes. When I opened them again, she was a tiny figure in the doorway, the floor tilting away like the deck of a boat at sea.

I was either sweating or shivering so bad my teeth chattered. Sometimes I'd see things clearly as movies on the air—a green parrot bigger than a man would look me in the eye and say,

"Cookies for breakfast, cookies for lunch." Sometimes it felt like my head and the room were the same size and so of course it was impossible for me to lift my head when my mother tried to slip some soup or water into my mouth.

One time I began shivering violently and then I saw it was because I was in the land of endless snows. A battle was raging, a city was burning. All the German soldiers had mustaches like Hitler and all the Russian soldiers had mustaches like Stalin. Sometimes the mustaches would fly off their faces and fight in the air like warring birds.

"I'll never complain about Dutch winters again," said Uncle Frans to me. His uniform was all torn and ragged and he was shivering as badly as I was. "Tell your mother that I'm coming home and to keep reading the old letters. I can't send any new ones. I'm out of stamps."

And the next time my mother propped my head up to spoon some soup into my mouth, I told her not to worry, Frans had just run out of stamps, that was why he wasn't writing her. He was alive and would be home soon.

But I failed to convince her. Later, when she had gone back down, I could hear her crying and saying over and over, "He's dead, he's dead, he's dead!"

My dreams started to last longer. They didn't disappear when I opened my eyes the way dreams usually do. They just waited there for me to come back and sometimes they'd even go on without me. They were all part of a bigger story and sometimes for a second I'd understand all the dreams and the big story they made, but only for a second.

I woke up and tiptoed downstairs. It was morning. The house was empty. I went out on the front steps, the door clicking shut behind me. There was ice on the streets but I wasn't cold. Everybody who passed was wearing yellow stars but when I looked closely I could see that instead of JOOD they had my name, JOOP, on them. They all waved to me and called out, "Joop, Joop," "That's his son Joop."

Then they all stopped, a thick crowd of them, which then parted to reveal Jesus Christ holding one of the twins in each arm, all three of them wearing yellow stars marked JOOP. When they drew near me Jesus Christ put down one of the twins and put his arm around me, saying, "I so love you, my son, that I give you the resurrection and the life."

The next time I awoke I knew it was for real. I didn't walk down the stairs on dream legs but on my own real legs, skinny and so shaky I could barely put one foot in front of the other.

When I looked out the front window, I could tell by the blue sky and the green buds on the trees that I had been sick a very long time, so long that the Russians had driven the Germans all the way back to Holland, judging by the sign in Russian pasted on our front window:

DIPHTHERIA

I turned around. And you, Willem, were sitting all alone in a high-backed chair glaring at me. Behind you in the doorway were our parents, who looked at me like a ghost, or a murderer.

17

When the quarantine sign came down and the neighbors brought us soup and bread, they spoke with surprise that one twin had died so quickly and the other had barely been ill. "Not as alike as people say."

The neighbors patted me on the head and smiled but I could see something else in their look, something I didn't like. To them I was the carrier of the disease, the one who infected his brother and survived fine himself.

My father had not worked during the weeks and weeks of quarantine. And not much after. Who wants a cook from a house with diphtheria? Our food supplies were thin, there wasn't a single coin in the cocoa can, the only thing we had in any quantity was the wood from the Jews' house, which warmed me through that early spring. I sat by the fire and wondered who I'd caught the sickness from—from someone I'd worked for, from sneezing Kees, from my father's cousin Helen. Sometimes I thought that the evil stinks I'd smelled in the Jews' house was a disease they'd left hovering in the air just waiting for someone to come by.

Returning to school was out of the question, I'd missed too much. As soon as I was back on my feet, my father took me to the office of his acquaintance, Mr. De Boer.

"I was working at his age," said De Boer, looking at me.

"Me too," said my father.

"School is good but you can't eat books."

"We may be eating them yet," said my father, and Mr. De Boer gave a little laugh. That just about seemed to clinch the deal but then Mr. De Boer looked straight at me and said, "Your father says you know the city."

I nodded.

"Where's Berg Street?"

"It's a one-block street, runs from Herengracht to Singel."

He looked over at my father and drew his jaw down to show he was impressed.

"And how would you get there from here?" he asked suddenly, as if trying to throw me off guard.

"From here?" I said, to buy myself a second to see the city like a movie in my mind.

When I told him the route I'd take, he looked puzzled, disappointed. "That's a dumb way. Why not straight over the Herenstraat Bridge?"

"Because there's a police post right there."

De Boer slapped his leg and laughed. "The kid's right," he said to my father. "I'm the dumb one."

I looked up at my father. He looked satisfied but I couldn't tell why.

"He's smart," said De Boer, "but has he got any meat on his bones?" He pinched my arm muscle, which I tightened as soon as I felt his fingers on me. "So you think I should give your boy a chance then?"

My father put his hand on my shoulder. "My Joop is a good worker, he'll be a help."

It was what I had wanted for so long—to feel his touch, to hear his voice speak praise of me—but now it only felt like he was selling me to De Boer.

"When can he start?" asked my father.

"I'll start him right now."

His hand still on my shoulder, my father walked toward the door, where he turned and bent down to me. "No stealing till I say so."

Stealing was the farthest thing from my mind, in the beginning I was so confused. Words like "back order" and "bill of lading" meant nothing to me, plus the warehouse workers had a slang all their own—"Gimme six bangers on a shorty." I was happy when somebody told me what to do in plain Dutch—load this, unload that, sweep the floor.

I was frightened of the Boss coming by and seeing me doing nothing, afraid he'd kick me out and send me home. So I started going up to workers and asking, "Can I help?" They started calling me "the Volunteer." Though they said it with scorn and laughter, it was good, it meant they'd noticed me, accepted me.

Now I could sit with them on the burlap bags and nobody'd think anything of it.

They didn't talk about the war much except to say how it'd screwed up their lives.

"If I have a good meal at night and a good crap in the morning, I'm a happy man."

"And when was the last time you had either?"

"Don't even ask."

Then someone else would say, "Me, I like a lot of things, beer, ham, and tits. But for sheer reliable pleasure, nothing beats a smoke."

"And when was the last time you had something worth smoking?"

"You can get whatever you want on the black market, providing you got the dough."

"Hide a rich Jew and you can smoke all you want," said a man I called the Rat because of his pointy features and because he took short steps but moved fast. He liked to make jokes about Jews, which made some people squirm and others laugh. I kept away from him.

Over time I figured some things out. Basically, we were a food distribution warehouse supplying stores with produce that people could buy with ration cards. But in any large operation there's always spillage and spoilage, not to mention pilferage. And so a certain percentage of the food ended up on the black market but exactly how, I had no idea, and nobody was about to explain such things to a kid, especially one who was stupid enough to keep volunteering.

It was cold in the warehouse because it was so huge. It made the job feel more lonely too. Not many people wanted to work with me. "Don't work too hard, kid, it could make other people look bad," said the Rat.

A lot of people did slack off. Sometimes I'd run across them sleeping in the upstairs bins, snoring on a pile of peas.

If there wasn't any work for me to do and no one would let me help him, I'd make up some work for myself, even if it was only dragging a sack of carrots from one place to another. I just had the feeling that if I stopped for five minutes, it'd be then that the Boss'd come around the corner.

But that wasn't the way disaster struck.

"Boss wants to see you first thing in the morning," said the Rat with a happy smirk, which I knew meant, "Bye-bye, suck-ass."

I couldn't look at my parents that night at the table. Twice my mother asked if I was feeling all right. I lay in my bed asking myself again and again what I had done wrong, but then I understood that it didn't matter—all it would take was someone speaking badly about me to the Boss.

It was late but I couldn't fall asleep. Every once in a while the light of a passing truck would flash across the ceiling. Finally, I figured out what to do.

I would pack my bookpack with clothes and take it to work with me. If I was fired, I would run away from home immediately. Go out to the countryside. I'd heard of people getting rides inside empty trucks that had brought milk into the city. I'd find a job on a farm and get through the war there until the country was freed by the English, the Americans, the Russians. Then I'd go home. My parents would take turns hugging and kissing me. "We thought you were dead. Our son, our boy."

I packed mostly warm things. It was already January 1944

and the days were short and cold. There was still some sand in
the bookpack from the time when Kees and I played saboteurs.

In the morning I tried to slip out of the house without the
bookpack being seen but nothing much got past my mother.

"What's that for?" she asked.

"I need it for work."

"For what?"

"The Boss'll tell me this morning. I can't be late."

"Then go."

I sat outside the Boss's office. Shadows flashed across the
frosted glass. Phones rang. Typewriters clacked.

I slung the bookpack over one shoulder when they called
me in.

"Aha," said the Boss. "The Volunteer."

"I work hard."

"I hear. I hear."

"I don't sleep in the bins like some people."

"Like my cousin Dirk," said the Boss with a snort of laughter. "Now listen, lad, here's the thing. We've got to make three
or four extra deliveries every day. You know the city, not just
addresses but how to get around. Interested in a little extra pay?"

"Yes, sir!"

"The only thing is that these deliveries are, how should I put
it, private, we don't want the Germans spoiling this business."

"How big are they?"

"Not so big, a kilo or two."

I was so happy not to be fired and to be given a chance to
make some extra pay that I was emboldened to make a sugges-
tion. "How about we make the deliveries around the time

school lets out? We can put them in my bookpack. I'll look like all the other kids."

For a second the Boss didn't say anything then came around his desk and pinched my cheek. He took out two guilders and shoved them in my hand, saying, "Give this to your father and tell him I thank him for sending me a worker so smart and so good."

". . . so smart and so good." I used the Boss's same words to end telling my parents how I happened to bring home two extra guilders.

"But I thought you said they told you to bring in your bookpack this morning," said my mother, more happy about the money than she was dubious about the story.

"I just didn't have time to explain it all this morning," I said. "What they told me was to come in with an idea and the bookpack was my idea."

"Doesn't matter," she said with a smile, going off to the kitchen to fetch dinner.

My father came over to me and leaned close. "Now," he said, "you can start stealing."

18

So, I stole. To obey my father, and to please him. But he never said anything about the amounts I brought home, never reprimanded me for bringing less than the last time, never praised me for bringing more. My mother always snatched the food from my hands—the sooner it was in her kitchen, the sooner it would be ours, not someone else's, not stolen.

The people I delivered the food to also snatched it from my hands and put it away fast, but for different reasons. The people who received these special deliveries were either rich enough to buy extra for themselves or were hiding people—Jews, young men evading German work details, or members of the resistance.

After a while I could distinguish those who were buying for themselves from those who were hiding someone from the Germans. It was almost like they had a different smell, the smell of people who loved only themselves. But who was hiding Jews, who young Dutchmen, and who people from the resistance, no way of telling that.

Right off from the way these people snatched the food from me and put it away, I could tell that they weren't going to be getting out their scales to make sure every last gram was there. On a good day I could steal enough peas to make a little soup and maybe a few small potatoes or beets that would make the difference between going to bed hungry or with just enough in your belly to fall asleep quick.

It wasn't easy work either. A bookpack loaded with beans weighed heavy after a while. I walked pretty much everywhere. By then bicycles had wooden tires or garden hoses wrapped around the rims. If you fell off a bike with a heavy bookpack on your back, you could crack your head good on the street. I walked everywhere, no matter how far or how nasty the weather. I earned what I stole.

Not to mention the danger. The Germans wouldn't exactly have patted me on the head for delivering food to people hiding Jews or resistance workers. By that late in the war everyone had heard about the torture cells in the Orange Hotel and the quick executions in the dunes.

I started putting a few books on top of the food in my book-pack just in case I was stopped by any Germans and told to open it up. I even got hold of a small NSB youth organization badge, which I pinned to my bookpack. But the Germans patrolling the streets didn't seem to give a damn about that or anything. They were older men, tired of everything, but still dangerous enough. Though the propaganda signs—GERMANY IS WINNING FOR EUROPE ON ALL FRONTS—were still plastered all over town, by early '44 everyone knew the Germans were losing the war. But the fighting still raged on the Eastern front and all we knew was that it wouldn't be over anytime soon. You could starve to death in the meantime, or get picked off by some disease. Rations were being cut, and so what I stole only got us back to where we were before.

The only good thing in my life was those two or three hours when I made my deliveries between the end of the school day and twilight. I was free of the huge, dreary warehouse and out in the city I loved. Any danger there was only made the city more vivid, the edges of the brick buildings crisp against the sky. The sad thing, though, was how grimy everything had become. Dirty windows reflected dirty canals. Still, life went on and you could see some of the things that always went on in Amsterdam, like the prostitutes with their bold eyes. And there were also things that had probably never happened before. One day I had come to a stop trying to remember which side of the trolley tracks the street I wanted was on when all of a sudden the building in front of me across the square just simply collapsed to the street. One minute it's there, the next it's gone in a cloud of dust. I found out the story later. When abandoned buildings were stripped for wood, support beams were sometimes taken. Then one day the whole thing just comes roaring down to the street in front of your eyes!

Once in a while I'd see a drunk who'd fallen into a canal. People would yell at him from the bridges and embankment, and usually the drunk'd yell back. It was always a good show. One of the old-timers at the warehouse even told me this was a city tradition. The only question was, said the old-timer, where were they getting enough booze these days to get that drunk?

Some of the city's drunks were real characters and were well known, usually for one special thing about them. One could sing the national anthem backwards, another could eat broken glass, and one called Proverb de Vries could quote you a good Dutch saying in response to anything you said to him. After four or five exchanges, you were expected to give him a coin.

It was De Vries who'd fallen into a canal one fine day in spring '44 as I was on my way to make a delivery of beans to Herengracht. People had gathered on a bridge and were yelling comments to him. Most of the time he'd reply with a proverb but sometimes he'd just tell someone to stick it up their arse. I didn't want to be late for the delivery but I didn't want to miss the show either. The bookpack was very heavy that day but I didn't dare take it off and set it down on the bridge.

De Vries's beard and hair were black as coal and he had a pointy chin that went up too high when he talked, like most toothless people. His eyes were so blue you could see them from the bridge.

"Better get out of the water before you die, De Vries."

"The young can die, the old must."

"Then you don't have much time, old man."

"Time is God's and ours too."

"You wouldn't be making up half those proverbs, would you now?"

"The world likes to be cheated."

It was just then that De Vries's eyes met mine. I had the strangest feeling that he was looking inside me, to check if I understood what he meant about death and God and time and a world that liked to be cheated. I felt dizzy and clutched at the rail.

I was brought back to my senses by the straps of my book-pack cutting into my shoulders. It was time to get going. Men were setting their wristwatches as the bells of West Church tolled five.

I had been to the address before a few times already. A nice old lady on the ground floor who always wore the same tan sweater would ask me in and give me tea by the woodstove. She was being truly hospitable, but it was also because she didn't want me going in and out of the building too fast—it might look like a delivery. When I left she'd give me some old news-papers and scrap wood "for your fire at home" but also because it wouldn't look right if I went in with a full bookpack and came out with an empty one. She was a nice old lady and wore the kind of glasses that made her eyes seem to swim like fish in a fishbowl, but she was a smart one, all right.

I felt a little bad about lingering on the bridge so long when she'd be waiting for me to come. Maybe there were other people there too, waiting for their food while I was busy watching a drunk in a canal. I quickened my pace as soon as I entered her street.

I must have been looking down as I strode toward her block because I didn't see the little crowd in front of her house until I was almost upon it. It was the police leading people out of her house into a Black Maria.

Just then I felt a strong hand closing around my arm from be-hind and I knew it was all over. She had told the police that a boy was coming with a delivery of food for them and they'd been just waiting for me.

"Don't move," came the voice from behind me. "Do exactly what I tell you."

I thought I knew the voice but was too scared to place it.

A few seconds later, his fingers still digging into my arm, he said, "All right, we're going to walk past the house and keep right on going, nice and slow, just two people who are talking and aren't that interested in seeing some more Jews arrested."

As soon as he said the word "Jews" I knew it was Rat from work. Still confused but a little less scared, I looked up at him as we started walking side by side.

"It's a good thing you're late," he said. "Otherwise you'd be taking a ride too."

Just then the police brought the old lady out of the house. She was wearing her tan sweater and big glasses. She saw me and smiled sadly. I looked up at Rat, who said, "Someone called us about the arrests and they sent me right over to look for you. The Boss was worried you'd get picked up too."

For a second I felt proud that the Boss was worried about me until I realized that what he was really worried about was me telling the police where I got the food I was delivering.

But then I found myself wondering if Rat had been the one who'd tipped off the police and had been waiting for me so I wouldn't arrive in the middle of everything and give away the warehouse's secret delivery system, which was how he discovered Jews in hiding and probably even got paid for that.

"What about the beans?" I asked him when we were away from the scene.

"Keep 'em."

"Won't the warehouse want them back?"

"They were paid for in advance."

So that day I returned home the Hero of the Beans. The kitchen suddenly became festive as my mother stored some of the beans and began cooking up the rest. The first whiff of abundance we'd had in years. My father stood in the doorway sipping ersatz coffee as I told the story in detail—the drunk who saved my life, the poor old woman in the tan sweater, and Rat, who might be all right but probably wasn't. I was telling the story to both of them but it was really my father I was addressing, not wanting him to think I'd done something dangerously stupid again by stealing much more than he'd ever meant me to.

There was a rap at the front door. I was immediately worried that it was the Boss coming for the beans; there was some mistake, they hadn't been paid for, Rat was wrong or lying.

"Get that, would you?" said my mother in a loving voice. She was still afraid to answer the door.

My father touched me lightly on the shoulder as I passed him on the way to the door but I could not tell what the gesture meant.

When I opened the door and saw Frans in uniform in a wheelchair, I knew at once, despite the blanket over his lap, that he had no legs.

19

"Hitler is shit! Russia is shit! War is shit!" shouted Frans, a glass of gin in one hand, a tear rolling down his cheek. "I was such an idiot. I thought war was romantic, heroic. You know what war's like? An explosion at a factory, an industrial accident!"

He suddenly fell silent, remembering something that made his eyes glassy. We were sitting at the same table we had sat at the night he denounced me to my parents, which had earned me the beating of my life and lost me the trust of my father. Maybe the circle was coming to a close now. I was now the Hero of the Beans and Frans was legless and weeping. Now he would no longer lord it over us but would be dependent on us for nearly everything—food, shelter, companionship. My mother's admiration for her brother turned to pity. My father took no pleasure in Frans's fate, only wishing that he hadn't been injured so seriously that we had to take him in.

"Near Stalingrad," said Frans finally, his eyes less glassy, "I came across two German soldiers with spoons in their hands sitting on the snow by a dead horse. They were spooning out its brains and eating them while they were still warm."

Frans had lost his legs when he was run over by a German supply truck when retreating from battle, not Stalingrad itself but something nearby. He'd been hospitalized in the Ukraine, screwups in his paperwork delaying his return home for close to a year. "They're not so interested in you once you've lost your legs and can't fight for the Reich anymore."

They weren't too interested in him back in Holland either. He got some veteran's benefits but it didn't come to much. Resources were stretched thin. Adult rations were around nine pounds of potatoes, two loaves of bread, a quarter pound of butter, and two quarts of milk a week. It was spring and so of course there was more hope around than in winter, and people like us could supplement our meager rations with vegetables from our little backyard gardens. With luck you could get through the summer but the next winter would be bad. No doubt it would be the last winter of the war and for some the last winter of their lives. That spring you could see how scrawny the children were when they started wearing their short pants and short-sleeve shirts again. Skin and bones.

Sometimes I'd go with Frans to collect his miserable benefits, helping him push the wheelchair up the bridges and over the broken paving stones. He always wore his uniform on those occasions. Some people gave him dirty looks, some people treated him with a touch of extra respect, but most people simply paid him no attention at all, too weary to care about anything but themselves and their own.

"I hate it when they look at my legs," said Frans, who always kept the blanket on his lap. "And I hate it when they look away."

Sometimes he screamed in his sleep in the middle of the night, waking up the whole household. My mother would go first to you, Willem, to comfort you, and then to Frans, who either yelled at her or wept. After a while my father would angrily call her back to bed.

If I couldn't get back to sleep I would go up on the roof and watch the British bombers returning home to England after a raid on Germany. The Americans had landed in June. Good, said people, but what took them so long? And would they be here by winter?

My father fell seriously ill that June. The doctor came and said the best medicine for him would be healthy food like eggs, which of course were no longer available except at prices that were astronomical. He could have just as well said, Eat diamonds.

Even with what I stole, even with Frans's allotment, even with our rations, we were slowly starving. Now we decided to each give a portion of our food to my father. It was then that we started eating tulip bulbs to make up the difference. Most Dutch didn't eat tulip bulbs before the "Hunger Winter" of '44–'45. We were pioneers. My mother would make a soup of them but we'd eat the bulbs too. At first they'd taste all right but after a while they started burning away the lining of your throat and belly.

After my father fell ill, my mother no longer comforted Frans when he woke up screaming in the night. She had enough to worry about and her patience was fraying. One night it snapped.

She had gone from my father to you, Willem, and then finally to Frans. But not to bring him water or comfort. To give him hell.

"It was you who brought the sickness into this house. You brought it like the nightmares that don't give us any sleep. You had to join the Nazis, you had to go to war. And what'd you get from it all? You've got less than you started with. And now you're killing us."

That night, wide awake in bed as my mother screamed, I vowed to kill Frans if my father died. It was Frans who had driven the first wedge between me and my father, and it would be Frans who'd prevent us from ever reconciling, prevent me from ever hearing my father speak my name again with love and pride.

I thought about ways to kill Frans. Stab him while he slept. Push his wheelchair into a canal. Or in front of a speeding German truck.

There were problems at work too. School was over now and so a boy with a heavy bookpack looked out of place and could draw unwanted attention. The Boss told me it was a good idea when I thought of it and it would be a good idea again in the fall when school started back up. I was mostly back working in the warehouse, which at least was cool on the hotter days. The coming of the warm weather also meant that stealing was harder. Not so easy to walk out with five hundred grams of peas or beans when you're wearing short pants and a light shirt.

It was all starting to affect me—Frans waking up screaming, my mother yelling at him, my father dying quietly in his room.

I wasn't getting enough sleep or enough food and was starting to make mistakes at work. Rat noticed. I was afraid he'd tell the Boss.

One day on the way back from a delivery that was legitimate, I saw people going into West Church and I went in with them, knowing it would be cooler inside, peaceful. I sat and prayed to God to save my father from death. I would give up anything. I would even throw my favorite jackknife with the bone handle into the canal if he would let my father live. When I was done I listened intently for a reply in the church's silence but all I heard was coughs and scuffling. I wasn't terribly disappointed because I hadn't really expected a sign then and there.

Just as I was leaving the church I saw a woman in a wheelchair who was having trouble making it over the threshold at the church gate. Her arms must be weak, I thought, as I grabbed the handles from behind as I'd done a hundred times with Frans and pushed her over the hump and onto the sidewalk. There was no rubber left on her tires, which made the going slower. She had a blanket over her lap like Frans but I could see she still had legs.

She never said thank you but, quick as a wink, she reached under her blanket and pulled out a tiny apple, which she pressed into my hand. I ate it in two bites, seeds and all.

I don't know why, maybe it was the coolness of the church or the sweetness of the apple, but I felt good by the time I got back to work. Rat gave me a wooden scoop and told me to fill sacks with peas. I liked the work, the sound the falling peas made, I liked seeing what you'd accomplished piling up before your eyes. I remembered everything that made me unhappy and it did not make me unhappy.

I even took a little nap behind a pile of sacks, the first time I'd ever done that. It was that thin kind of sleep, so thin you can hear sounds through it, but still dark and restful. When I woke I looked around to see if anyone might have spotted me but the warehouse seemed quiet, almost deserted, even the sunlight on the cement wall seemed to have come to a halt. And it was then and there, sitting on a mound of peas, rubbing my eyes, that a great idea came floating through my mind. In one second I was on my feet.

20

Frans sat in his wheelchair by the canal looking at the water as I told him my idea. We would use his wheelchair to make deliveries. Even the Germans wouldn't lift up the lap blanket of a legless veteran. He liked the idea. It would put him back in his sister's good graces, help improve the family's food supply, and maybe even stand him in good stead after the war. Yes, he could say, I did join the German Army to fight the Communists but I paid for that with my legs, and when I came back to Holland I helped Jews and resistance fighters in hiding.

"But Jews are shit too," he said, still looking at the water. "And so are resistance fighters. You know what resistance means for most of them? A German soldier walks by, they put their hand in their pocket and give him the finger. And then after the war, the stories they're going to tell! And people like me will be kicked around by those same shits."

That was just his way of saying he agreed. But he did have one objection. "The tires on my chair are just about shot. It'll be hell on my kidneys, you pushing me all over the city. We'll need some better tires."

"But where can we get them?"

"I've got a friend in the furniture business," he said with a grin.

On the way Frans told me that he used to make fun of his friend Piet for working in the *Hausraterfassung* tracking down Jewish property that had not been declared, everything from copper bowls to furniture to automobiles stored in some farmer's stable for the duration. "Don't be a pencil pusher, I'd tell him. Come to Russia and fight with me."

Piet was waiting for us outside his warehouse. He could not control the sadness on his face when he saw Frans. For a moment he wasn't sure how to greet him. First, he extended his hand then leaned forward to give Frans a hug.

"You were the smart one," said Frans to Piet, who was pushing him up the ramp now, me walking beside.

The warehouse was huge but mostly empty. There were a few dozen wheelchairs in one corner, all tagged and lined up by size.

"Where's everything else?" asked Frans.

"Shipped to Germany a long time ago. We did our work too well. Put ourselves out of a job."

"I thought Jews are sent to labor camps," I said.

"They are," said Piet.

"What kind of work can cripples do, especially if their wheel-chairs are taken away?" I asked.

For a second Piet didn't say anything. "They must give them new wheelchairs there. Frans, let's see if we can find some decent tires for you now," he said, peeling his wire-rim glasses off. They left red creases on his nose and the sides of his head.

"They still pay you even though there's no more furniture to be found?" asked Frans.

"We still find some. And now they pay us for Jews, thirty-seven fifty a head. If there's ten thousand of them in hiding, that's three hundred seventy-five thousand guilders' worth of Jews."

"That's money!" said Frans.

"There's about fifty of us on the case."

"You go out looking?"

"Mostly we depend on tips."

"The informant get any money?"

"Officially, no . . . ," said Piet, with a tone that meant for old friends there's always exceptions.

"I should have stayed home in Holland," said Frans, pinching the rubber tire on a wheelchair like a housewife testing fruit at the market.

I parked Frans outside the warehouse where I worked. I was a little smarter this time and negotiated with the Boss. "If I could figure a way to make some good-sized deliveries with practically no risk, would you pay me three guilders a delivery?"

"Why three guilders?"

"It's the price of two eggs. The doctor said my father needs two eggs a day."

"Tell your father I wish him a speedy recovery."

"I will."

"What's your idea?"

I explained it to him, pointing to Frans through the window. "You got a head on your shoulders, Joop, you can tell your father that too."

The dispatcher gave me the address of a grocer's shop on Leliegracht and told me to ask if Mr. van Hoeven had been let out of jail yet.

"Is that a password or a real question?" I asked.

"Both."

When I asked at the store everyone just shook their heads. Not another word was spoken. They took delivery of ten kilos of peas.

That evening I handed my mother two eggs. She smiled at them. "One tonight," she said briskly, "and one tomorrow."

I watched from the doorway as she fed my father the egg, telling him I was the one who'd brought them home. She had to lift his head from the pillow.

When she was leaving, still clicking the spoon in the empty cup, she whispered to me, "No closer than the door."

Then I was alone with my father. There were so many things I wanted to say to him that I couldn't say any of them. Just as I was about to turn and leave, I saw his lips moving to form words. I leaned closer without quite leaving the doorway.

"Even," he said, "even the Queen wakes up hungry."

21

I fell asleep happy. I woke up happy. I had even slept happy.

It was my father's words that had filled me with happiness. "Even the Queen wakes up hungry." They were words that had meaning only for us, even my mother wouldn't have understood what they really meant. And what they really meant was that there had been days when he and I had walked through the food markets together, when he had taught me the things he knew, when he was proud to introduce me as his son.

With those words he was thanking me for helping save his life. He wasn't hating me anymore. I was his Joop again.

And my mother loved me that morning. She smiled as she prepared the second egg. Frans, at the table dipping bread in tea, was deferential: "Do you want me today?"

"If there's any work for us I'll come back by and get you."

The only one who did not show me any special feeling that morning was you, Willem. You stood in the doorway looking at me, not with anger, not with interest, just waiting for me to go.

It was a beautiful day, early July. If you didn't look too close, the city looked almost clean and beautiful again. Except in the old days the streets were packed with cars and bicycles. Now they'd mostly been confiscated. Now there were only cabs that always made me laugh—horse-drawn cars with their fronts chopped off. You couldn't get a pint of gasoline. A cousin who came in from the country told us about the local countess who was always driven to church by her uniformed chauffeur. When the gas was gone, she'd have him, still in uniform, drive her to church on a bicycle built for two. We got a laugh out of that one.

But there were some problems at work. A delivery of shelled peas had arrived in rotted burlap bags that had split apart when handled. The floor was ankle deep in peas. It was all hands on deck.

Even though it was no real emergency—the peas weren't going to go rolling away, and so what if they got a little dirty from the floor? We all pitched in, working fast and furious, using brooms, dustpans, scoops, whatever we could lay our hands on. A few people slipped and fell, which was good for a laugh.

One of them was Rat, who didn't think it was so funny. He lay on the floor grimacing for a minute, trying to determine if he was all right or not. But lying on the peas was no pleasure either and he hopped back up onto his feet. Dusting himself off and still wincing, he said to me, "Boss wants to see you."

"Soon as I'm done here."

"Right away."

It must be some important delivery, I thought. I should have brought Frans with me. Now I'll have to run all the way home.

But as soon as I was in the Boss's office I could tell it was something else. His face was flushed and it wasn't approval that flashed in his eyes.

For a second he didn't say anything, as if not quite sure how to begin. I could tell that he was very angry but that he still liked me and was even in some strange way a little afraid of me.

"Joop," he began, "yesterday when you came to me with your idea, you didn't tell me how your uncle lost his legs, isn't that so?"

"Yes, sir."

"And it was only last night that I found out that he lost them fighting with the German Army on the Eastern front."

"That's true."

He shook his head. "That is not the sort of person I want making special deliveries for us, can you understand that, Joop?"

"My uncle doesn't care about any of that NSB stuff anymore. Since he lost his legs he says everything's shit."

"Well, there are still some people in Holland who don't think everything's shit."

I nodded.

"Your uncle's worse than a fox in the henhouse and I won't have it. You come back with your bookpack when school starts."

"But that's—"

The phone rang. He picked up the receiver and signaled me to leave by flicking his fingers at me.

It was all God's fault and Frans's. If God hadn't sent me the idea of using the wheelchair when I was in church and the old woman slipped the little apple from under her blanket, and if Frans had just been run over by a tram car in Amsterdam like a good Dutchman and not gone to fight the Russians, I wouldn't have been laid off.

Now we were worse off than ever. The little I was paid and the little I could steal would be lost to us for at least two months. I didn't know how I was going to tell my mother what happened. I decided I wouldn't tell her. I'd get up every morning and pretend to go to work. Maybe in the course of the day I could scare up some work or steal some produce so that it'd look like I was still employed. But how could I get the sadness off my face? I was on the verge of tears. I sat in a park and tried to start crying to get it out of me but it wouldn't come.

But I couldn't go home until the end of the workday. I trudged all over the city and could manage to swipe only one cucumber.

Frans was sunning himself in front of the house when I returned home.

"Didn't need me today?"

I shook my head.

He grabbed my arm. He could see that I was sad and scared.

"What happened? Tell me!"

For a second I resisted but then it all came rushing out—the story, the tears.

Frans relaxed his grip on my arm and stayed silent for a few seconds. Then with a mournful grin he said, "Only the Jews can save us now."

22

"Get eggs," said my mother as I left for work the next morning.

"I can't get them every day."

"Get eggs."

I went out into the city. It was hot and reminded me of the days when Kees and I went tramping around looking for a German vehicle to sabotage. And after a few hours I had the same feeling of futility I'd had back then. Nobody wanted help, nobody needed work. And there wasn't a single chance to swipe so much as a cucumber.

I sat down under a tree by a small canal. I would have no lunch that day, I might as well have shade.

I tried not to think about food. I tried to think about how to find some Jews we could turn in to Frans's friend Piet and split the reward. Then we could buy eggs for my father, a cucumber for me. So I ended up thinking about food anyway.

I kept dozing off. I'd wake up and see a barge go by on the canal then nod back off again, dreaming of white bread and peacetime.

When I finally woke up I could feel that the bark of the tree had pressed its pattern into the skin on my back while I was sleeping. Now I stretched and yawned, aware of the emptiness in the pit of my stomach.

"Even the Queen wakes up hungry"—my father's words echoed in my mind. At first, all I felt was sadness. Those were the words he'd used as a joking reminder of our good times together and to say that his love for me had never really died out. I did not want those words echoing in my mind and tried to move away from them but they kept tugging me back. They would not let me go until I had fully understood them.

If even the Queen wakes up hungry, Jews in hiding must do the same.

Food was the trail that would lead to the Jews.

The grocery store on Leliegracht where I'd delivered the ten kilos of peas was the obvious place to start. They accepted "special deliveries." That meant they then either delivered them or people came by to pick them up.

Suddenly, the taste of futility was gone from my mouth and the hunger from my belly. I had a destination, a purpose, a chance.

I felt like a detective. Watching the store while trying not to be noticed. It was a quiet afternoon. No deliveries came to the store and none went out. There were a few customers but none of them bought much. Finally, just as I was about to quit for the day, a big stout red-faced woman went into the store and quickly came out carrying two bulging shopping bags.

I decided to follow her. But then I started to worry—what if she was hiding resistance fighters? I didn't want to turn in resistance fighters. It was wrong. And they'd get you back for it. And Piet didn't say anything about the Germans paying money for fighters, only for Jews.

But I must not have been that good a detective because it wasn't long before she stopped, wheeled around, and said, "What are you tagging after me for?"

"Can I help you carry?"

"I look weak?"

I kept walking behind her.

"Didn't you hear me?"

"This is my way too."

Just then four or five little children came out of the front door of a house, calling, "Mama! Mama!" A minute later two bigger boys came out. She wasn't hiding anybody. Just feeding a big family.

Still, I wasn't discouraged. I had my plan and new ideas were already coming to me. When I turned onto my street I saw Frans in his wheelchair in the same spot he'd been the day before. As I approached, he beckoned me over, holding up his cupped hands. I walked over. Smiling, he opened his hands. An egg.

"Eggs," said my mother the next morning as I pushed Frans out the door. I knew what she meant. One egg was not enough to keep my father going. Not to mention us. We'd had tulip bulb soup again for dinner the night before.

My head was full of the kind of math problems they give you at school. If it takes two eggs a day to keep a sick Dutchman alive, and if an egg costs 1.45 guilders on the black market, and if a Jew in hiding turned in was worth 37.50 guilders that would be split fifty-fifty with the informant, then how many Jews did it take to keep a sick Dutchman alive for a month?

But the real problem was where to find those Jews. Frans agreed that we should start by keeping watch on the grocery store on Leliegracht. "They didn't arrest that grocer for nothing," said Frans. "And we know the store's still receiving illicit deliveries. We made one."

The problem was that we were conspicuous. There was an old woman who lived above the grocery store and sat by her window all day. She'd noticed us. She did not turn away even when I stared back at her.

Whenever we felt that we'd been on that street too long, I'd push Frans over to West Church, where there was good shade. We'd rest and talk about ways of improving our chances. We agreed that for the time being at least, it would be smarter not to go hang around any of the private homes where I'd made deliveries in the past. They might have lookouts who'd recognize me and know no delivery was scheduled. There had been a case just recently of a resistance fighter shooting a known informant in the head as he was working a neighborhood. And the neighborhood we were working was bad enough—the people in the grocery store had already seen us once and the old woman was at her window every day.

The air was hot, dusty, still. To keep from getting bored, I pretended to be a famous detective, Frans my trusty assistant. We looked for clues—people carrying large bundles of food, people who might be Jews going around the city with forged papers. Frans said you could always tell Jews by a certain look in their eyes, a mix of fear and superiority.

We had no luck following people leaving the grocery store with large bundles. Either they hopped on bicycles and were gone in a flash or else we could follow them and, like the stout woman, they just turned out to have big families. "Eight kids is nothing," said Frans. The only luck we had was with German soldiers or NSB. Frans would strike up a conversation with them and some of them would give him a little food or money.

So, for the first couple of weeks we did manage to bring home a little something—bread, margarine, a few eggs, even a little chocolate—better than nothing but not enough to keep five people going. My father was slipping away again.

One evening I stood in the doorway of his room, which smelled of piss and sickness. For a long minute he seemed to stop breathing. Tears came to my eyes. And then all of a sudden he started breathing again and I bawled like a baby.

My mother no longer said "eggs" when we left in the morning. She didn't say anything. And there was nothing we could say either.

Frans and I always tried to get something to eat at a street soup kitchen so we wouldn't come home too hungry and there'd be more for my father.

Sometimes Frans and I would split up when we got to the neighborhood around Leliegracht. Especially if I was following someone who didn't look 100 percent Dutch. No way we could keep up if I had to help Frans with his chair.

When Frans was by himself, people would come up to him and ask if he needed help. Conversation sprung up naturally. Frans found out the little things about a neighborhood that only the people who lived there knew. And of course there'd be the occasional coin.

It got so that I could tell from a distance just when Frans would be telling someone his story about the German soldiers eating the horse brains in the snow.

One day I came back after following a dark-haired woman and saw a policeman talking to Frans. I had a moment of fear. Had someone reported us?

But then Frans saw me standing there and beckoned me over.

"This is my nephew," he said to the policeman. "He helps me get around."

"Good boy," said the policeman with a nod at me. "You wouldn't believe what kids his age and younger are doing these days. Breaking in all over the city and taking whatever they can get their hands on. Hunger's driving people crazy. Everything's up—murder, burglary, stick-ups. And prices."

"But not a soldier's pension."

"Or a policeman's pay."

"Say hello to your wife."

"Take care, Frans."

"I knew him from before the war," said Frans when the policeman had left. "Look what he gave me. Ration coupons for bread and milk." Now we just had to find a store that hadn't already run out.

The next day I saw my first dead person. It was very early morning. I was pushing Frans across a bridge. "Look," he said, pointing to the canal. It took me a second to spot it and at first I couldn't tell if it was a tire or a suitcase. But it was neither. It was a man. A pretty fat one at that, floating facedown in the water.

" 'Course it could be a drunk who just fell in the canal and drowned, but I don't think so," said Frans. "Booze's too hard to come by to get that drunk plus which, the guy's pretty fat and winos're skinny. No, my guess is he was a Jew in hiding who died in the night. And that of course would have thrown the Dutchman hiding him into a panic. Bad enough to be shot for hiding a live Jew, but who wants to be shot for hiding a dead one, especially since that also means he's stopped paying.

"It could even be a Charlie Chaplin movie. This little scrawny Dutchman trying to get this enormous fat dead Jew down the stairs without getting crushed and then across the street to the canals without getting picked up by the Germans," said Frans, laughing. "Oh, that's a movie I'd pay to see."

The last days of July were very hot. No rain fell. The heat made you lethargic. That, along with the lack of food.

Sometimes I'd be standing behind Frans's chair and just doze off. One hot day I dreamed that the canals were frozen over and waiters on skates brought their customers cold glasses of gin on silver trays. I blinked my eyes and opened them and that scene was gone but what I saw was almost as startling. Kees was standing right in front of Frans's wheelchair staring at him and me.

I smiled, happy to see him, the first time since we'd gone out shoveling together, to warn people against Maarten, just before I got sick. "Kees," I said.

But there was an angry sneer on his face that said, I see who you're siding with now. Before I could say anything he trotted away. I knew I should run after him, explain, tell him how sick my father was. But he never loved his father like I loved mine.

"Ah, the other saboteur," said Frans, remembering where he knew Kees from.

I stayed where I was.

The doctor said he wouldn't come. He had no medicine and we had no money. He asked what we were feeding my father and when we told him he just shook his head to say it was hopeless.

Hopeless was just how I felt on the last day of July '44, sitting with Frans in the shade of the old trees by West Church. Frans was dozing. I was awake, but what I saw around me had no effect on me, like a movie I couldn't understand. And so I did not pay much attention to the old woman who walked past us until she suddenly turned around, marched over to us, and began speaking so sharply that Frans was awake at once.

"What do the two of you want on my street? I see you there every day."

Only then did I know who she was, the old lady who sat by the window above the grocery store. But up close she didn't look so old even though her hair was gray.

"What do we want?" said Frans. "What everybody wants—a bite to eat, a little luck."

"There's nothing left to eat in Holland. And our luck ran out a long time ago," she said with a fury that was frightening. "Yours too, I see," she added with a look at Frans's legs.

"That's right, mine too. In Russia. There it's even worse than here. I saw German soldiers eating horse brains with a spoon."

"Serves them right," she said. "But you at least came back alive."

"True," said Frans. "You lose a husband?"

"Him I lost before the war. No, a son."

"How?"

"The Germans took him for forced labor at a plant in Hannover, Germany. The British bombed the plant. So, you tell me, who should I hate, the Germans or the British?"

"Hate the Jews," said Frans. "If it wasn't for them, Hitler wouldn't have started the war in the first place."

"And I do hate them," she said. "Especially the ones with money who went into hiding so they wouldn't have to do forced labor like my boy."

"They always use their money to wriggle out."

"And don't think they aren't eating better than the likes of us while they're in hiding."

"How do you know that?" asked Frans.

"I live above the grocery store and I watch what goes on. The owner used to deliver potatoes himself. He wouldn't send the errand boy, no, he'd bring them himself, who ever heard of such a thing? One day I went out and watched where he went."

"And where would he bring those potatoes?" asked Frans.

She paused for a long second, either trying to remember or deciding whether to tell. "Prinsengracht," she said. "Two sixty-three."

23

In the dark the corner of a table jabbed me in the ribs. I tried to cover my mouth with my hand but was a half second too late. I stopped where I was, waiting for the pain to go away and to see if the noise I'd made had roused anyone in the building, *if* there was anyone in the building.

Using his connections, Uncle Frans had found out that before the war the building at 263 Prinsengracht had belonged to a German Jew named Frank. When his older daughter was called up for labor service in Germany in July 1942, the whole family left at once for Switzerland. But they may have only pretended to leave Holland and might still be living in the building, or had let other Jews stay there. Either way, nighttime was when they'd be up and moving around.

I'm not sure if Frans had made some deal with the warehouseman but it seemed like some of the door panels had been loosened. I didn't want to do the break-in but Frans said I had to. His friend Piet would do only one raid on our say-so and if they came up empty-handed, that'd be the end of that. And we were doing it for my father, weren't we? said Frans. And who was supposed to do the break-in, him in his wheelchair?

Once the pain wore off some and I was fairly sure that no one had heard me cry out, I started moving slowly through the dark, my arms stretched out like a sleepwalker's.

But I didn't get more than ten steps when a creak from somewhere above brought me to a halt. And what if it wasn't Jews in the house but resistance people who'd cut your throat in the dark and worry about how old you were later? I told myself that all old buildings creaked in the night, our house did, and not every sound meant someone coming to get you.

Sliding one foot slowly after the other, I made my way forward, toward the stairs. I had taken a last look at my father before I left the house. He was sleeping. His face seemed so small. I pictured him as I inched forward. I was doing it for him. For him.

But then something ran over my foot—too big for a mouse, too small for a cat. It had to be a rat. I had a horror that one would run up my pant leg. Now I couldn't move forward no matter how much I pictured my sick father's face.

But I did have the strength to turn and leave. I could just tell Frans there was nobody there, nobody at all. We'd have to find our Jews elsewhere. We wouldn't hurt our chances with Piet. I was so scared I even started hating my father for being sick and making me do things to take care of him when he should have been taking care of me.

Then all of a sudden, just as I was about to turn around and slip back out the way I came in, I had the clearest image of your face, Willem, before me. I don't know why, I practically never spoke to you or gave you a moment's thought, but there you were clear as could be in the darkness of the room, and though the face was gone in one second and never said a word, I could tell from the expression in your eyes that what you wanted to say was, You killed my brother, now save our father.

That pricked me back into action. I put one foot in front of the other. I listened for any scurrying sounds but everything was very quiet now. Even the floorboards had stopped creaking. That made my own breathing sound too loud to me. I paused at the door to the stairs until my breathing had slowed a bit.

The stairs were steep and narrow. I reminded myself to crawl back down sailor-style, facing the stairs. Three-quarters of the way up, I paused to listen again. It wasn't the dead quiet of an empty industrial building. More like a house where people were sound asleep.

Now I was on the third floor. But what now? Keep exploring in the dark? This time if I bumped into something, somebody was bound to hear. There might not be time to get away if I moved too far from the stairs. I decided to stay put for a while.

After a few minutes, my eyes started getting used to the dark a little. Now some things were darker than others. I could see the dark outline of my hand in front of my face. There was a bookcase, and the large books in it were darker than the spaces between them.

I told myself just to sit down and wait. If there was anybody there, I'd hear them. Sooner or later people made sounds, no matter how quiet they tried to be.

In the mystery stories the great detectives sometimes had to wait for hours. Even days.

But I had to wait for only about twenty minutes before I heard a soft sound coming closer and closer. Light footsteps from behind a wall. Then the bookcase in front of me began to open slowly like a door. Then it stopped. I thought I heard a girl's giggle. A second later the bookcase door opened fully. A white robe seemed to be floating through the air like a ghost. It was coming right at me. Now I could see it was a dark-haired girl in a nightgown. A voice from the floor above called softly but sharply, "Anne!"

The white robe stopped and turned then floated back and closed the wall behind her.

I was so scared I wet my pants.

PART II

24

"I don't believe it!" said Willem angrily.

"Don't believe what?"

"It wasn't me who appeared to you in Anne Frank's house. That was just your own mind. It wasn't me. Not the real me."

"But it was the real you who ate better after we got paid by Piet. We all ate better, our father, our mother, you, me, Frans. That probably gave us some reserves to get through that last winter, what they call the Hunger Winter, when children were dropping like flies. Could've been you, could've been me, but it wasn't, it was other kids. And your own kids and grandkids, they wouldn't be in the world if you hadn't made it through that last winter. So, you can say what you want about the Willem who appeared to me, but the Willem who sat down at the dinner table, that was you, no two ways about it."

"But why should I believe a word of it?" said Willem, almost rising from his chair. "You can't prove any of it. Who can back you up on it? Uncle Frans, Piet, everyone else, they're all long dead. Who knows, maybe you're cracked. Maybe the war cracked you and you never got over it. Or maybe you did turn in some Jews for the money but now you're just pretending that it was Anne Frank to make yourself feel important and make me feel bad. Or maybe you didn't turn in any Jews at all. Maybe our father just got through the winter."

"And maybe Uncle Frans came back from Russia with both his legs and Jan never died."

Willem made a movement, the beginning of an objection, but then let it drop.

"This is not the story I expected to hear," he said finally, his voice softer. "Not at all."

"I never thought about it all for years," I said. "I had too much to do after the war. Taking care of my father, *our* father, taking care of myself. There was no Anne Frank yet, her book wasn't published until years after the war. And then when it was published I did hear something about it, but I didn't make any connection. Then one day I turned on the television and there was a documentary about her and it mentioned her address, 263 Prinsengracht, and I knew in a second."

"And how did you feel?"

"Angry. Unlucky. I mean, something like twenty-five thousand Jews went into hiding. And something like ten thousand were betrayed for one reason or another. Not the best record, nothing to be proud of. Maybe Amsterdam should erect a monument to the Betrayers to remind everyone how horrible people can be.

"You know what happened to all the Jews who were betrayed? Pretty much the same thing. Sent to the Dutch transit camp at Westerbork and from there to Bergen-Belsen, Teresienstadt, Auschwitz. Then death from typhus or gas. Their names are still on the lists the Germans kept and on the memorials the Jews built, but other than that, who ever heard of them?

"And who ever heard of the people who turned them in? They've probably forgotten it themselves. If you reminded them, they'd say, Maybe it did happen, all sorts of things happen in wartime, that was more than half a century ago.

"They were the lucky ones. No one gave a shit about their victims. But mine has to leave a book that half the world's read. I've got the worst goddamned luck in the world. For years I kept waiting for them to come for me—some cop, Nazi hunter, historian, or reporter running down the facts one more time, hoping to make their name off the dead girl. But they never came. They never came close.

"After a while nobody's really trying that hard, especially the Dutch. They like things the way they are. Three-quarters of Holland's Jews go to their deaths, worse than Fascist Italy, but thanks to Anne Frank the country has a reputation for heroism, resistance, humanitarianism. Why tinker with that? Why arrest some old Dutchman and open up that stinking can of worms, especially with all those free-spending tourists coming to smell the tulips and see the Rembrandts?"

For a while we just sat in silence, drinking. I went to the kitchen and came back with a bottle of gin. This wasn't a beer conversation anymore. After the first gin, I asked, "And so did our mother ever talk about me? Did she ever tell you any stories about me at all?"

"Of course, she did, of course. A lot of what you told me, I'd already heard from her—how happy the soap you brought home made her, she used to say that was the only truly happy moment she could remember from the entire war. And she talked about the cocoa can where you threw the coins you earned, how proud she was of you for that. And how worried she was when Uncle Frans caught you and the other boy, what was his name?"

"Kees."

"Kees, pouring sand in the German Army truck. No, she told me stories, but less after my sister was born, and less, of course, after she got sick, she was only forty-four when she died; you and me, we've both lived so much longer than either of our parents," said Willem with sorrow, though his eyes were still wary.

"Our father never spoke of you," I said. "Or of our mother. To him, I guess, you were both the same, the ones who left him at the worst hour. He did keep a picture of you and your brother by his bed, but it was facing away from him, more for the nurses and visitors to see."

I could see that hurt him. But it was the truth. Except that he hadn't asked.

"I was all he had left," I continued. "And so at last I got what I always wanted, his love, his attention. But it was in such a terrible way that I could not be happy about it. Still, it was better than nothing, and he was all I had.

"I used to bring him the little beef tartare sandwiches on the buns that he always loved and I'd even give him a few sips of beer from a bottle hidden inside my jacket. My turn to give him a few sips."

"You have such stories," said Willem, looking down at his

glass of gin and shaking his head. "Things no one could have ever imagined. Like what you told me about me and Jan fighting over the Jewish stars in the park."

"You know, I read a book about the German occupation not too long ago, a good book, and it said that lots of children liked the stars, thought they were pretty."

"And did you ever read her book, Anne Frank's, the diary?" asked Willem

"But wait a second," I interrupted. "You told me that our mother talked about me to you, told you stories about me, but all the stories you mentioned, the soap, the cocoa can, Kees, were stories I just told you. How can I believe that my mother ever said anything to you about me if you only tell me back my own stories?

"I want you to remember something else, some other story she told you."

For a second Willem looked very worried, but I couldn't tell whether he felt caught in a lie or was afraid he wouldn't be able to remember any of her stories on demand.

"It's been so long . . . ," he said, looking off. "But give me a minute, I'm sure something will come."

To give him a chance to think I got up and went to my bedroom to get the girl's diary and my glasses. The book was full of colored strips of paper to mark passages and I had even made notes on some of the slips.

I had been gone only a minute but Willem seemed a bit startled by my return.

"Any luck?" I asked.

"Not yet."

"Did our mother ever hear from her brother, our beloved

uncle Frans?" I said, a little interested, but more to jog his
memory.

"You know, I can't remember her ever much mentioning
him. Maybe she said something about him going to the Dutch
East Indies after the war, but I can't be sure. How about you,
you hear anything?"

"Not much more. He went off to stay with some friends in
the south of Holland just before the liberation, but I don't think
we heard of him again."

"Wait, that reminds me," said Willem, sitting up straighter in
his chair. He had a way of fiddling with his glasses, making several little adjustments until their positioning was just right, maybe
a professional habit, like a barber smoothing his hair. "We moved
from Canada to Oregon then to California. Our mother liked it
there. She used to say that what she liked best about California
was that nothing there reminded her of Holland, not the
weather, not anything. One day I came home from school and
found her sitting at the kitchen table with a cup of coffee she'd
barely sipped, looking a million miles away and like she'd been
crying or might cry any minute.

"I put my hand on her shoulder and asked if she was OK. She
nodded that she was, but she nodded her head too quickly and
too many times. I knew she was thinking of Holland and the
war but it couldn't have been the weather reminding her, it was
another perfect California day, blue sky, no clouds, eighty-five.

" 'It's Joop's birthday,' she said. 'And I got to thinking about
him. How brave he was during the war, going out for money,
eggs. I never really told him how brave I thought he was because his father stayed mad at him and thought he shouldn't be
overencouraged or else he might do something stupid and dan-

gerous again. And, even worse, I never told him that I didn't blame him for little Jan's death. I never said those words to him.' And then she started crying."

For a few seconds I didn't say anything, taking a long, slow sip of gin. "But you could have just made all that up to make me feel good. That's not the kind of story I wanted to hear. I wanted to hear a story our mother told you about me, a story with little details in it, like the time I brought her home a little blue pitcher with a white cross on it from a burned-out house or the time we were crossing Rembrandt Square together and one of the black marketers bought her a cup of real coffee because she was 'Joop the runner's mother.' After that she called me 'Joop the runner' for a while. If you told me stories like that I could know they were true. But just some malarkey to make me not feel bad about Jan's death—well, I never felt that bad about it, I almost died myself, didn't I? That's not the kind of story I wanted to hear."

"And you think the stories you've told me are the kind I wanted to hear?"

"Mine are true," I said. "But what you told me about my mother, maybe she said it, maybe she didn't."

"And maybe Frans came back from Russia with both his legs and little Jan never died."

25

We each drained a long gin in silence then I said, "You ask me if I've read the girl's book. I have. I'll tell you how it happened."

I still walk the streets of the city but I don't love it like I used to. Amsterdam's less than half Dutch now, I read that in the paper. Indonesians, Moroccans, Turks, Surinamese, more Muslims than Christians. But the good thing about walking is that sooner or later it makes you hungry, and hunger takes your mind off your problems. Maybe it was my stomach directing my feet because as soon as I turned onto Spui Square I knew what I was going to eat, the same little beef tartare sandwiches my father loved, the specialty of a little snack bar called Broodje van Kootje.

Raw hamburger, raw egg, raw onion, salt and pepper, on a

little bun, washed down with a Palm beer on a cool spring day, that puts me right with the world.

My father had loved it so much when I'd brought them to him in the hospital. His eyes would light up. "Tartare" was one of the few words he'd say in all those years.

I looked out at the square. Students swooped by on bicycles. Pigeons scattered so they wouldn't have to bother flying. Two bickering tourists kept turning their map, trying to figure out where they were. I saw everything but what was right in front of me, the Athenaeum Bookstore. And as soon as I saw it a heavy-hearted weariness came over me. I knew that today I would buy the girl's diary.

In the bookstore I had that feeling of strange amazement—that what's so clear to me is so invisible to others. I didn't ask for help but the book wasn't hard to find. It's like everything else these days, on a shelf, for sale.

The cashier smiled at me as women do when they see a man doing something they approve of, pushing a baby carriage, carrying flowers.

"Would you like a little bag?"

"Yes, please, I would."

Walking quickly back across the square as if leaving a disreputable place, I fought the temptation to open the book and read a few lines at random and treat those lines as prophecy or judgment. No, no, wait till you get home, then read it like any other book, start to finish.

But that didn't help. After avoiding the book for years and years, I suddenly couldn't wait to open it. Why not just check to see if there's any mention of the peas I delivered to the grocery store belonging to that van Hoeven who'd been arrested himself by then? I'll just check that and won't look at anything else till I get home, that's the deal.

I'd made that delivery sometime in the first half of July '44. The entry for Saturday, July 8, 1944, seemed to be about nothing but strawberries, twenty-four crates of strawberries. ". . . Father ended up making jam every evening. We ate hot cereal with strawberries, butter milk with strawberries, bread with strawberries, strawberries for dessert, strawberries with sugar, strawberries with sand. For two days there was nothing but strawberries, strawberries, strawberries . . ."

All those strawberries while my father was starving in his bed and we were eating tulip bulbs.

But then in the middle of that entry for the same day, I found what I was looking for: "Mrs. van Hoeven has let us have some peas, twenty pounds!"

It had to be the same twenty pounds I delivered.

Anne Frank ate them. They gave her strength, energy, nourishment. So, I helped her live, not only die. That must be counted in my favor.

26

What's so great about her book? I don't see it. A moody teenager, boy-crazy, she hates her mother, who cares?

And spoiled! She gets the twenty pounds of peas, with no appreciation of the danger people went through to deliver them or that the delivery would cost someone, me, his job. All she can see is the inconvenience to her in shelling the peas. Wait, I'll read you her own words: "Stripping pods is a precise and meticulous job that might be suited to pedantic dentists or finicky spice experts, but it's a horror for an impatient teenager like me . . . My eyes were swimming: green, green . . . The monotony was killing me. . . . When I stopped, I felt a bit seasick, and so did the others. I napped until four, still in a daze because of those wretched peas."

Her own Jews are dying right and left, people like my family are clinging to life by the skin of their teeth, and she's going on about those "wretched peas."

She's not even suffering. She says hiding's like "being on vacation . . . there's probably not a more comfortable hiding place in all of Amsterdam. No, in all of Holland." Nothing but the best for her family. And she thinks it's all fun and games. "I look upon our life in hiding as an interesting adventure, full of danger and romance." She wouldn't say that if she were watching her own beloved papa wasting away under a dirty sheet. She wouldn't say that if she came out of a long illness to find her own sister dead. She wouldn't say that if she were eating tulip bulbs instead of green peas.

She's a snobby little rich girl who makes lists of what she's going to buy after the war and who'd turn up her nose if she passed me on the street. She can't wait to get back to her usual high standard of living, complaining that they've been using the same oilcloth to cover the table since the war started. "How can we, whose every possession from my underpants to Father's shaving brush, is so old and worn, ever hope to regain the position we had before the war?"

She thinks everything about her is interesting—to people and to God. "Sometimes I think God is trying to test me, both now and in the future." But that's not how God works.

How God works is like this. Anne Frank wants to be a famous writer. She prays for it. "If God lets me live, I'll achieve more than Mother ever did. I'll make my voice heard . . ." But if she lives, she'll just be another teenager who hates her mother. It's death that makes her famous. God answers her prayers for fame. He sends her death. He sends her me.

She gets fame. I get a secret.

Sometimes Anne Frank sits by the window in the hiding place at 263 Prinsengracht and peeks out through the heavy curtains at the street and the children of the neighborhood "so dirty you wouldn't want to touch them with a ten-foot pole. Real slum kids with runny noses." Like me they wore "thin shirts and wooden shoes. They have no coats, no socks, no caps and no one to help them. Gnawing on a carrot to still their hunger pangs, they walk from their cold houses through cold streets to an even colder classroom."

Maybe I was one of the ones she saw go by. It could be, everybody uses Prinsengracht. Anyway, it's the Anne who sits by the window I feel closest to. She says, "Our thoughts are . . . like a merry-go-round, turning from Jews to food, from food to politics. By the way, speaking of Jews, I saw two yesterday when I was peeking through the curtains. I felt as though I was gazing at one of the Seven Wonders of the World. It gave me such a funny feeling, as if I'd denounced them to the authorities and was now spying on their misfortune."

Now I like her. Now we're friends.

27

Around then I started talking to Anne in my mind. Maybe I am cracked like you say.

I say things like, I've started circling by the house on Prinsengracht where I saw you that one time, Anne. It's all different around there now. By the canal across from West Church next to a pissoir there's what they call a Homo Monument. And right beside the church is a fancy new restaurant. There's also a statue of you that looks nothing like the photos of you in the book. Japanese teenagers have their picture taken there. And around the corner on Leliegracht where the grocery store was, the one the nosy old woman lived over, there's an American bookstore and a fashion shop for pregnant women.

The whole town smells of fresh paint. Too spiffed up for my taste. More for foreigners and gays. It's not our Amsterdam,

Anne, not wartime Amsterdam, when everything was sad and thin, even the air.

I go by late at night or early in the morning before the Anne Frank House opens and the long line of people forms. It costs seven euros fifty to get in. They've turned you into a saint and a business.

Sometimes at night I sit in the Café Westertoren. It's jolly there, always lots of dogs and laughter. The tourists don't come in. One look inside and they're on their way—too many drunks with bruises on their foreheads, though they're more from falling than from fighting. The bar girl is saucy and the gin is cheap.

Still, from there I can hear the bells of West Church, heavy and serious when they toll the hour, the bells you liked to listen to during the war. Through all the shouting and music of the bar I listen to those bells that tell me another hour of my life is gone and whatever's waiting up ahead is that much closer now.

My life is nearly over and I've never really lived. I died about the same age you did, Anne. The secret kept me from people, from life. I could have buddies, not friends. Whores, not a wife.

I'll be going to your house soon, but not quite yet, I'm not quite ready yet. A few more days, this week, within a week. It's not something you want to rush. It's important. So you want to do it on the right day, that makes sense, doesn't it?

It's not that I'm afraid something will happen in there, what could happen? At worst I could get claustrophobic and go running out. But strange things do happen. The other night was warm and I sat outside. I could feel the sound of the bells vibrating in my rib cage. I noticed a woman more or less my age sitting alone at another table, smoking in an odd way, taking several quick puffs then seeming to forget all about her cigarette and drink. She'd drift off. She was nicely dressed in an artsy sort of way. Hair dyed dark brown. A little lipstick. Then she'd snap out of it, take a sip of her drink, and another several quick puffs. Once she got out a pen and a little pad of paper and wrote something down. I thought it was you if you'd lived.

It's a nice day, warm even. Why people would want to go to a museum on a day like this is beyond me but the line's already around the corner when I arrive.

The dark paint on the doors of 263 looks old. I like that. But they don't let you enter there but in the modern building to the right of it. I get in line. The air is full of the sound of cell phones and foreign languages. A big group of teenagers in sneakers, baggy pants, and caps on backwards is lining up. They could be American, they could be from any country. The adults with them aren't dressed much better. During the war even the men in line at the soup kitchens wore hats and ties.

The line lurches and halts, lurches and halts. The couple in front of me have a quick, intense discussion and leave the line for some other attraction, the Van Gogh Museum, Rembrandt's house. Now there's a young man in front of me. He has green South Sea island tattoos on the side of his neck. That has to hurt, no matter what drug you're on.

We're around the corner now. A big sign warns tourists to beware of pickpockets. On the museum a sign says no backpacks or baby strollers will be allowed in; they can be left at

Centraal Station. But I can see that people with backpacks are being let in, not like the ones I had as a kid, but made of materials that didn't even exist then, rayon, Velcro.

If I'm going to bail out I better do it now, the line's almost to the door. Once you're in, it might be tricky getting out. Maybe somebody'll want to know why I'm leaving all of a sudden.

But nothing's going to happen inside. You'll see the house again, this time by day, with a line of tourists, and it won't mean any more to you than the sight of the house you lived in as a child. You go there, you stand, you look and you look, and nothing happens.

Inside, television monitors show old newsreels of Hitler ranting, German paratroopers over Holland, Jews wearing yellow stars, roundups, death camps. The pictures are accompanied by a teenage girl's voice speaking in English. It's supposed to be Anne Frank, but then why isn't she speaking Dutch, or at least German?

All the newsreels are in black-and-white. These modern kids must think the past happened in black-and-white. Sometimes it does feel that way.

Nobody's too interested in the warehouse part of the building where Otto Frank's business was located. His company dealt in spices and pectin for making jam. There's a quote from Anne's diary on the wall as there is in every room: "I don't think Father has a very nice business. Nothing but pectin and pepper. As long as you're in the food business, why not make candy?" Which makes me realize we were all in the food business, her father, my father, me.

The air is bad in here. It must have been like that for them all the time. People are already fanning themselves with brochures.

And then all of a sudden I'm in front of that steep staircase I first climbed more than sixty years ago when my legs were much shorter but more flexible for that.

The young man with the tattooed neck is already mounting the stairs, the people behind me are pausing in respect for my age. In a second or two they'll be politely asking if I could use any help.

But I start up the stairs, which, fortunately, are so steep that all your attention goes to where your foot is now and where it's going next.

Now I can see that there are two large windows on the landing beside the bookcase that swings open. I did not notice them that first time, they would have been covered with that special blackout paper we all grew so heartily sick of during the war. But maybe some light did seep through the blackout paper; it stays light till almost eleven in summer, maybe that's why I saw the white flash of your nightgown, Anne, before the woman's voice called you back up.

Uncle Frans had told me, "If you hear women's voices, that means there's Jews in there. The Dutch hiding from doing labor in Germany are all men. Listen for women's voices. Women mean Jews."

My heart is beating awfully fast. I don't know if it's the memories or the stairs. If it's a heart attack, let it be quick. But my heart is fine. A little clammy sweat makes my shirt stick to my back but other than that I'm fine. In fact, it's the young man with the tattooed neck who doesn't look so good, fanning himself with a brochure.

There's nothing left in the rooms you all hid in. After a raid, big moving trucks marked PULS would come and take the furniture away; that's what must have happened here too. All that's left are your movie star photos pasted to the wall, Garbo, Ray Milland.

Two years in this place, I'd have gone crazy, no air, no getting away from the other people, the stink of them.

Maybe the one good thing about getting arrested was that for a while, at least, you were back in the open air.

There is a sign that says:

THE ARREST. AUGUST 4, 1944.

THE HIDING PLACE HAD BEEN BETRAYED.

NOBODY KNOWS BY WHOM.

Not quite nobody.

But then I think, maybe the sign is right because who's the real betrayer? The nosy neighbor who told Frans and me about the special potato deliveries to 263 Prinsengracht? Or the worker in the warehouse at 263 who loosened some of the panels in the door? Or me, who broke in and heard women's voices, which meant Jews? Or Uncle Frans, who told Piet? Or Piet, who made the call?

Everybody's glad to be free of those empty, airless rooms and be back in the twenty-first-century lobby, where everything is crisp and clean and on the computer. They have the computers set up in clusters of three at little stations. The ten-year-olds seem best at working them. Maybe it's me, or maybe it's my machine, but the 3-D images of Prinsengracht do not come floating by on my screen. I twirl the ball, press the buttons, but nothing moves, nothing happens.

But I do like the little video theater where you can vote yes or no, green or red, about various "situations," as they call them. They show little movies. Skinheads. Soccer fans shouting, "Hamas, turn on the gas." A Dutch politician speaks out against immigrants. A woman of Islamic origin calls Mohammed a "pervert." What's more important, freedom of speech or people's feelings? Some of the choices are tough. It's interesting for a while.

But then my mind wanders. I make up my own little movie for you, Anne. You've got a choice. All you have to do is nod your head and my father will die in his bed in early August 1944. He was close to death anyway, and it wouldn't have taken much to push him over the edge. So, all you have to do is nod your head and he dies. And that means you save your whole family's life, your mother's, your sister's, your own, and the lives of the people you were in hiding with, and the life of your beloved father, even though he was going to survive anyway, the only one. You can save them all from the gas chambers and the crematoriums and the mass graves where you and your sister will be thrown. My father's not going to live that long anyway, and if he dies now I won't go out looking for Jews with Uncle Frans, we'll scrape by on soup kitchens.

If you love life, if you love your family, if you want to save me from the sin of betraying you, nod your head.

And you do nod, Anne; in my little movie, you do nod.

PART III

28

"But, but," said Willem, sputtering, "but you just did the same thing you did with your other story about going into her house."

"What do you mean?"

"The night you broke into her house during the war, you were just about to leave after the rat ran over your feet, but then all of a sudden you have a vision of me and that gives you the strength to go on. Now you go back to her house after all these years and this time it's Anne Frank you're seeing, and she's telling you she'd have done the same thing in your position."

"But those kinds of things happen to me. They've been happening to me ever since I was a kid. Since the day I had a beer with my father and went outside and felt God taking notice of me from the other side of the sky."

"Just because it's been happening for a long time doesn't mean there's anything to it. It's just part of a story you tell yourself to get yourself off the hook."

"Nothing gets me off the hook."

"And so you want me on it there with you to keep you company?"

"You don't like my story, make up one of your own."

"At the very least I need a cover story. You know, there's a bunch of guys, good guys, I play squash with once, twice a week. Afterwards, we sit in the sauna and shoot the breeze. They're going to say to me, So, how was the trip? Did you find your brother? What was he like? What did he tell you about your childhood and the war? They know why I went, what I was looking for. I can't bullshit them, my friends sitting there naked in the sauna; I can't bullshit them. They'd know in a minute."

"So," I said, "you're going to need two stories. One to tell yourself, one to tell them. Probably can't find one that does both."

"I've got an idea!" said Willem, glad to be the one telling the story for a change. "I'll say I found you, it took some tracking down but I finally found you in an old people's home in Haarlem or Delft and your memory was pretty shot, so I only got bits and pieces. But some of them were good, I'll say, and I'll tell them about you getting caught by Uncle Frans and the yellow stars and the cocoa can. That'll be enough. Nobody's that interested in anybody else."

"How about your granddaughter, the one who's so interested in her Dutch heritage, what if she wants to come over and meet what's left of her uncle Joop?"

"I'll tell her you don't want to see people anymore, it's too much of a strain. And besides, she doesn't speak Dutch."

"But what if she defies you like those young Americans are always doing and comes here and finds me and sees that I'm not in a nursing home in Haarlem but living on my own in Amsterdam, then she'll know a big lie was used to cover up something else, and that something else had to be big too."

I could see my little scenario—defiant youth, search for roots, the hidden truth—worried him. He drank down his gin, gestured for a refill, then smiled. "I don't think that's ever going to happen but if it does, you can always say something like there were some shameful things you didn't want her to know. You and Uncle Frans did spend some time looking for Jews to turn in but you never did, of course. You had good reason to try, our father being so sick and all, but you never did."

"So then how did we get food to live through that summer, that fall, that terrible winter?"

"I know! You remember that hot day you were in front of West Church and dozing off from hunger behind Uncle Frans in the wheelchair and you were dreaming of skating waiters and then you opened your eyes and there was your friend . . ."

"Kees, Kees . . ."

"Yes, your friend Kees, and so instead of him turning away from you, now he says he's been looking for you everywhere because he's working for the underground and you can help him warn people hiding Jews who are about to be raided. The German cops aren't about to stop a kid pushing a war vet in a wheelchair and so, if you help out, you and your family will get double rations. You'll get eggs and be a hero too."

"I wonder what happened to Kees," I said, more to myself

than to Willem, and for a second I felt the old fear of Kees, the fear the cowardly liar feels when he has to face the brave one not afraid of the truth.

"That's a pretty good story to tell other people," I said. "But what is the story you're going to tell yourself?"

"I don't know yet. But I do know that whatever it is, I'll have a secret that will keep me separate from everybody, my wife, my kids, my friends, everybody, till the day I drop because I can't be known as having anything to do with the girl's death. I don't want to be *that* to people."

"But you'll be *that* to yourself."

"To yourself is different. Bad enough, but different."

"Look, Willem, nobody asked you to come here. You had everything, our mother, America, a new life, and I was stuck here with the shit. Now you know what the story was and you don't want it. You can't tell it to your wife, your kids, your friends. You want me to lie for you. You're going to turn me into a drooling idiot in a nursing home or a fake resistance hero for your granddaughter in case she ever comes over and finds me. But I'm not either of those things. I'm just the guy who stayed. Who dealt with the shit and the truth. And now I'm supposed to start lying to protect my American brother, who doesn't like how the story turned out and wants to return it for a better one like a defective appliance."

Willem was stung into silence. He stared into his glass of gin.

"And how about this little story, Willem—one day there's a knock at your door in California and guess who's at the door? Uncle Joop, over from Holland, wanting to meet his long-lost relatives, you must be Tommy, you must be Cindy. Sure, if Willem can turn up on his brother's doorstep in Amsterdam, why can't Joop return the favor? And then, of course, they'll be looking at you funny because you said Uncle Joop was drooling away in a home and here he is hale and hearty. What's going on? What's the real story?"

Willem was still silent.

"You wouldn't want to live in fear of that happening, would you? Wouldn't the truth be better than that?"

"No," said Willem, "the truth is worse than anything."

29

Still and all, Willem, I want to thank you for coming, for finding me. It's a terrible thing I've carried all these years, and so just to have a chance to speak of it was a relief and a blessing.

A few times I came close to telling my story to some stranger, a whore, a fellow passenger on a train or ferry, but something always held me back.

Now I'm glad of that. To tell the story to a brother, a person who was . . . there and a part of it, that's so very much better.

I don't think our mother and father ever knew anything about it. Uncle Frans wouldn't have told them. Our mother was just grateful to have some money and food. By that late in the war no one asked where things came from.

So, only Frans and I knew, and then he disappeared, he had plenty of reason for that. That left me.

But now you know. We were never really brothers when we lived under the same roof. You and Jan never liked me and you liked me even less after Jan died. The only good days I remember were the days with the yellows stars in the park. And there weren't that many of those. And then, of course, you were gone for the last sixty years, so what kind of brothers can you say we are?

At least that's the way I felt when you first came and we started talking. But I don't feel that way now. Now that I've told you the story. Now that you know the secret. We're brothers now, brothers of the secret.

Don't take it all so hard, Willem. Let me tell you something: it turns out no matter how bad your secret is, you can live with it. In a way you even get used to it, like, I don't know, like a lump on your arm. You get to know its shape; some days it's more painful than others, sometimes you can even forget about it for days on end. Not that you don't always come back to it. It's where you start and where you finish.

Some days it would be painful and I'd be hating the secret and I'd say to myself, Would you rather go blind if the secret would go away, would you agree to lose both your legs if the secret would go away? I thought about that a lot. And in the end, you know what I decided? Maybe one eye, maybe one leg, but not both.

I feel bad that the girl died young, but our brother Jan was much younger and he barely got a chance to see the world.

He got the disease from me, I'm sure of that, but who did I get it from? Some other person who didn't mean for Jan to die any more than I meant for the girl and her family to die.

Of course, I can't lie and say I didn't know what happened to

Jews, especially Jews who'd been in hiding. I heard what Frans said, what other people said, even the girl knew, it's in her diary, she knew they were gassing them.

But we were too tired and hungry to be thinking about what might happen to people we didn't know and had never seen.

If anyone's to blame it's God, that's what I sometimes think.

Do I believe in God?

Only fools think there's no God. And only fools think God is good.

When I was a kid I read stories about Dutch sailors off in their small boats at sea and how all of a sudden everybody'd go silent as they all felt something gigantic pass beneath them, a whale that could smash them to smithereens without even meaning to.

I felt God on that day when my father gave me beer and praise and I went outside and felt something on the other side of the sky taking notice of me.

And when I prayed to God on the day my father had started to give me the second beating but was interrupted by the *razzia,* who else gave me the idea to go back downstairs to the cellar?

And then when I was in West Church I helped the old woman in the wheelchair and she pulled out the little apple from under her blanket, which gave me the idea to use Uncle Frans and his wheelchair for deliveries.

Why hadn't the woman in the wheelchair eaten her apple earlier or given it to some other kid who'd given her a hand?

And using Uncle Frans for deliveries was a great idea but then it turned out to be not so great because it got me fired, so then we had to find Jews to turn in so my father wouldn't die.

And that busybody old lady who sat in her window all day,

why did she have to spot us and come over and be charmed by Uncle Frans so she gave us the address against her better judgment or whatever it was that made her hesitate at that moment? I can still feel her hesitation after all these years.

And God could have sent another rat over my feet when I was in the house at 263 Prinsengracht and scared me away once and for all.

You know what I sometimes think of doing? I sometimes think of writing a letter to the International War Crimes Tribunal in The Hague to say you should stage a trial for God in absentia because he is the greatest war criminal of them all.

Either God saw everything that was happening and didn't care, which makes God guilty of criminal negligence. Or else God took an active part in it all, giving me ideas, not stopping me when he could, which makes God an accomplice. Either way he's a criminal, a war criminal.

Come on, God, tell us, which one was it, it's just me and Willem here, a couple of drunk brothers, you can tell us, which one was it?

Then, of course, there was silence. There were little sounds, my breathing, the drip of the faucet, cars passing. But still it was silence. The silence that always comes when you ask God for something. Not just any silence. God's.

Then there was another silence. Ours. The silence of two people who had said everything there was to say and were just waiting a decent interval.

This time at the door, Willem and I each slung an arm around the other's shoulder.

"Your story," said Willem, "it was true, right, all of it?"

"Would I lie to my own brother."

1. Is Joop responsible for Anne Frank's death? Partially? Fully? Not at all?

2. Does Joop feel enough remorse for the suffering he helped cause?

3. Is Joop's brother Willem partially responsible for Anne Frank's death? Joop points out that Willem did eat the extra food they got for betraying Anne's which might have saved him from death during the terrible last winter of the war.

4. Should Joop have done anything possible to keep his father alive?

5. How do you understand the dream Joop has when he is ill with diphtheria? Is it mere delirium? Or does it have meaning? Or is it a mix of meaning and delirium?

6. How does the quote from George Orwell help you understand the book?

7. What is the role of food in this novel?

8. Does the book exploit the memory and image of Anne Frank, or is it a sincere attempt to understand what motivates people during wartime?

9. Why did Uncle Frans became a Nazi?

10. Who do you think the mysterious couple is that Joop met in the park, and what was in the package he delivered for them?

A Reading Group Guide

For more reading group suggestions, visit
www.readinggroupgold.com.

St. Martin's
Griffin